# Advance Praise for
## *The Dawn of a Nazi Moon*

"Powerful women breaking every glass ceiling possible in a quest to defeat an unworldly Nazi threat in a high-stakes battle of the space domain. I love it."

—JEANNIE KRANZ, former Senior Congressional Space Advisor
and Space Executive

"MacKinnon has long dealt with 'Deep State' issues. They don't get any deeper or more mysterious than this book."

—MARTY MARTIN, former Senior CIA Operations Officer
and Special Forces Operative

"Douglas MacKinnon combines a background in government with the writing skills of a novelist. And so he's produced a lively and thought-provoking story which serves as a useful reminder that we'll face unexpected threats and surprises in the near future."

—WILLIAM KRISTOL, former White House Chief-of-Staff
and Director, Defending Democracy Together

"Truly chilling. Real-world and alternative history and space technology blended into a jaw-dropping, can't-put-down novel."

—CAPTAIN WILLIAM F. READDY, U.S. Navy (Ret.),
three-time space shuttle astronaut and commander

# THE DAWN OF A NAZI MOON

book one

## DOUGLAS MacKINNON

PERMUTED
PRESS

A PERMUTED PRESS BOOK

The Dawn of a Nazi Moon:
Book One
© 2020 by Douglas MacKinnon
All Rights Reserved

ISBN: 978-1-68261-914-8
ISBN (eBook): 978-1-68261-915-5

Cover art by Cody Corcoran
Interior design and composition by Greg Johnson/Textbook Perfect

**PERMUTED PRESS**

**Permuted Press, LLC**
New York ✦ Nashville
permutedpress.com

Published in the United States of America

For my wife, Leela June

Simply put,
she *is* the joy and happiness finally reached
on that journey called life.

# 1

## May 1, 1945

During the waning days of World War II, in a desolate corner on Peenemünde—the most fanatically guarded facility in Nazi Germany—SS General Heinrich Kemmler looked out at the ten most advanced scientific creations in the history of the world.

He smiled to himself as he squinted out the window of a massive fortified cement blockhouse two miles away and fought to visually locate his creations through the falling rain and the rapidly approaching darkness of night. "Actually, it's just one creation replicated ten times," he thought out loud.

As he stared out the window, the general knew that Russian troops were just days away from taking the base and torturing and killing them all.

For that reason, weeks earlier he had evacuated chief scientist Wernher von Braun, the chief scientist's younger brother Magnus, and a majority of the two thousand or so other Nazi rocket scientists to central Germany, next to the Mittelwerk factory.

The general did this for two reasons: The first was to keep Nazi Germany's top rocket scientists out of the hands of the savage Russians. The next, and more important reason, was to keep secret from those very scientists—men and women he considered less than loyal to the Führer and the Third Reich—what he and his team of handpicked SS scientists had been working on and finalizing for the last number of months on direct orders from Adolf Hitler himself.

If only the world knew.

But, General Kemmler thought to himself, that was the whole point. The world would *never* know what was about to happen, in mere minutes.

* * *

ALMOST EIGHTEEN MONTHS earlier to the day, General Kemmler had been summoned to Hitler's heavily guarded private home, the "Berghof on the Obersalzberg."

The Obersalzberg was a small mountain located just outside the picturesque Alpine town of Berchtesgaden on the Bavarian-Austrian border.

Several years before, General Kemmler had arrived for the most amazing and surreal meeting of his life. Hitler's bootlicking subordinate Martin Bormann had set about completely transforming the town from a peaceful village into a retreat for the upper echelon of the Third Reich.

The truly psychotic Bormann accomplished this by evicting every resident in the area—while gleefully executing those who protested in the least way—and then destroying their farms, homes, and businesses.

In their place, he erected a Nazi Shangri-La, where the senior members of the regime enjoyed Alpine chalets built within walking distance of the home of their beloved Führer.

In addition to the chalets were hotels for invited guests, a massive garage to house Hitler's car collection, a schoolhouse, a state-of-the-art movie theater, several teahouses—including the infamous Eagle's Nest—and even a lavish greenhouse to cater to Hitler's strict vegetarian dietary habits.

Beyond that luxury, and even more importantly, Bormann built a number of highly fortified barracks to house Hitler's personal crack SS unit, which had two jobs, and two jobs only: protect Hitler at all costs, and kill anyone—and their family—who remotely posed a threat to the "god on Earth."

A task they not only relished, but salivated to carry out.

It was into that town and that atmosphere, again, that General Kemmler found himself years later at 4:00 p.m. on a Friday afternoon.

After going through multiple checkpoints and two invasively thorough searches, he was escorted into a relatively small but ornate sitting room that housed several easy chairs, a large fireplace, and a conference table for six people.

Thirty seconds after he entered, a door at the back of the room opened, and Adolf Hitler slowly strolled through with his hands folded behind his back. Following him in quick fashion, like an eager-to-please puppy dog, came Martin Bormann.

Kemmler had only personally met Hitler once before, when the Führer had summoned him and Wernher von Braun to Berlin for an unscheduled update on the V-2 rocket program.

But then, as before and now, General Kemmler, brilliant as he was, had an incurable blind spot regarding the Führer. A man his own father served with and spoke highly of during the Great War. For whatever reason, Kemmler truly came to believe that with Hitler, he was in the presence of either a god on Earth or a mortal sent down by God to save Germany and the Fatherland from the nations and mongrel scum of humanity bent upon its total destruction.

Because Kemmler was certain that Hitler was a conduit and speaker for the word of God, he knew it was his duty to obey that voice and its commands to the letter of the law handed down to him from above.

But, even if that were not the case—a dark thought Kemmler allowed to barely exist in the deepest recesses of his mind—and Hitler was indeed a crazed man as some of his fellow officers whispered in the shadows, far away from the ears and the informants of the Gestapo, he was still the leader of Germany and of the Fatherland—a country and a vision that, as a professional soldier, Kemmler had sworn to protect and defend…at any cost.

Hitler stopped in front of the large fireplace and let the roaring and flickering yellow flames warm his back as he studied his six-foot, three-inch, impeccably uniformed general. As he did, a hint of a smile moved the ink-stain-looking smudge of a mustache a millimeter up his haggard face.

After the heat from the fireplace removed the chill from his hunched body, Hitler simply nodded once toward the highly polished conference table.

Kemmler went and stood behind one of the chairs, but did not pull it out and sit until the Führer had settled himself into the cushioned chair at the head of the table.

As the two men sat, Kemmler caught sight of Bormann moving to stand in front of the fireplace, and then not so discreetly picking his nose and wiping his stained finger on the side of his already soiled pants.

As much as Kemmler believed in all that Adolph Hitler represented, he hated just as much the non-soldiers like Bormann and Nazi Minister of Propaganda Joseph Goebbels. Bormann, Kemmler knew, was literally a convicted murderer who weaseled his way to the side of Hitler and became more and more insane with each passing day. As for Goebbels, Kemmler viewed him in even a lesser light, if possible, only because Goebbels was highly intelligent and accomplished but still chose to turn himself into a shameless opportunist in the pursuit of more and more power.

General Kemmler had no such desire for power. None. He only wished for the victories Hitler envisioned, and felt that fawning bottom-feeders like Bormann and Goebbels distracted from and even prevented those goals from being realized.

Hitler softly cleared his throat, and Kemmler immediately averted his eyes from the nose-picker back to the Führer.

"Thank you, General," said Hitler softly as his unblinking eyes looked upon Kemmler, "for coming on such short notice."

"Of course, my Führer. It is my honor and my duty."

Hitler nodded slowly and then turned his head slightly in the direction of Bormann still lingering by the fireplace.

"Martin. We are about to put all of our faith into General Kemmler today. Is that not so?"

The rat-faced Bormann turned to look first at Hitler and then at the professional soldier who, truth be known, made him feel inadequate and much less of a man.

"Indeed, my Führer. And I am positive that he won't let us down."

"No," replied the megalomaniac leading Germany to ruin. "No, he won't. The general is not only beyond loyal but quite possibly the most gifted and intelligent officer in my army."

Of that, Hitler was entirely correct. A fact that would eventually prove fatal for the Allies.

General Kemmler was about to be molded into the arming device for the ultimate time bomb. One created and activated by Hitler on this day in history—one that would not go off for years or even decades in the future.

# 2

Hitler swiveled in his chair to better face the general and take some of the pressure off his weak neck and spine.

"General," continued the Führer. "As you know, I have been working tirelessly to bring the Fatherland all that it is owed and deserves. While the ultimate mission is still the Thousand Year Reich, in which the Aryan race rules supreme while cleansing the world of all inferior species and threats, a great leader must also prepare for...*all*...possible outcomes. It is that reason and more which brings you here today."

As a number of scenarios instantly began to flood the general's already on-edge mind, he wisely chose to bite his tongue and simply listen.

Before Hitler went on, he unexpectedly, very angrily and very loudly rapped his right knuckles on the table while making a motion with his left hand at Bormann.

The henchman for the Führer instantly scurried over to the table and sat in the chair to the left of Hitler.

Hitler turned his head and stared hard at Bormann for a good five seconds.

As he did, General Kemmler made a point of carefully examining his own fingernails before brushing an imaginary piece of lint off the right cuff of his jacket.

All great leaders, Kemmler knew, were eccentric to some extent, and as Hitler was the greatest leader of them all, he was entitled to his bizarre behavior from time to time.

After several more seconds, Hitler turned from Bormann to look back at the general, with now a slight smile on his face.

"As I was *saying*…my ultimate goal is the survival of our master race. Survival, for *centuries* to come. To help ensure that, I created an elite team to not only scour the Earth for rare, historic, religious, and even supernatural artifacts, but to also identify places around the world where we can plant our 'seeds' to sprout at a later time. A survival tactic that I am about to expand. And expand in a way the mind cannot comprehend."

General Kemmler did indeed know of this elite unit. He knew of it because one of his most trusted lieutenants had been recruited into it one year prior.

Over a quiet dinner at the general's home six months after he had been recruited, the lieutenant privately, confidentially, and quite excitedly told him all about the unit and his own growing role in its top-secret mission.

The elite unit was called the *Ahnenerbe*—which literally translated into "Inheritance of the Forefathers." It was created in July of 1935 under the direct orders of SS head Heinrich Himmler, and then monitored continually by Hitler himself.

The Ahnenerbe's overriding assignment was to find the relics that most fascinated Hitler. Among these were the *Ghent Altarpiece*, a painting Hitler was convinced contained a coded map to the most sacred of all Catholic relics, the *Arma Christi*, or the instruments of Christ's Passion: the Holy Grail, the Crown of Thorns, and the Spear of Destiny.

Hitler truly believed that the possession of the Arma Christi would grant him supernatural powers as well as immortality.

General Kemmler knew that Himmler had long been fascinated by the occult, and that he had transferred much of that interest to the Führer himself over the last number of years.

An interest Kemmler found both curious and quite disturbing.

With his dinner still untouched, Kemmler's lieutenant confirmed all of that background and more as he went on in jaw-dropping detail.

Soon after the Ahnenerbe's creation, Himmler had held a secret meeting at the Wewelsburg, the dreaded castle headquarters of the SS. During the meeting, he officiated the very first initiation ritual for twelve super SS "knights" modeled after the Arthurian legend.

In addition to that initial band of knights, Himmler assembled a small army of psychics and astrologers whose main mission would be to try and poison the minds of the enemy while simultaneously planning battle tactics for the Third Reich that would be based upon the alignment of the stars.

Beyond that, the lieutenant reported that Himmler was "growing" a laboratory of "super soldiers" pumped full of not only steroids and other human growth hormone drugs, but literally the DNA of centuries-old Germanic warrior "heroes" extracted from the skeletons and mummified remains within their final resting places.

The lieutenant then breathlessly revealed how he and other team members had already been to Ethiopia in search of the Ark of the Covenant, to Tibet in search of the mythical Yeti, to Languedoc to try and unearth the Holy Grail and the Spear of Destiny, and most importantly, to Iceland to locate the secret region that housed the *Thule*—telepathic giants and fairies that Hitler was positive were the true ancestors of the Aryan race. Hitler was certain that the Thule not only had the power of flight, but telekinesis and telepathy as well. Powers, Hitler concluded, that were eventually lost because the Thule were discovered and made the mistake of mating with "lesser" races.

Hitler instructed the Ahnenerbe team members that the recovery of DNA related to the Thule was his most sought-after prize, because with that DNA, he could re-create a "master race of gods here on the planet Earth. A master race which…"

Another loud rapping of knuckles on the table snapped General Kemmler's mind back to the present.

A present that found Adolf Hitler leaning across the table with his face just one foot from Kemmler's.

"Am I boring you, Herr General?"

Kemmler instantly realized that his mind had strayed into the details of the Ahnenerbe much longer than the few seconds he had imagined. With Hitler now just inches from his face sporting his well-known maniacal stare, Kemmler felt his pulse quicken and adrenaline begin to seep into his bloodstream.

Kemmler did not have to be reminded that Hitler had others he felt had offended or insulted him executed in the most gruesome of ways.

"No, my Führer. Not at all. The opposite in fact. In my excitement of being in your divine presence, my mind wandered trying to guess my purpose here."

Hitler sat back in his chair and contemplated the response without once breaking his stare into the eyes of the general.

"Your value to me…and the Fatherland," Hitler said ever so slowly, "takes precedence at the moment. That said…value can be a fleeting commodity, my dear General."

"Yes, my Führer."

Hitler suddenly clapped and rubbed his hands together and broke out in a smile that displayed his uneven and yellowed teeth.

"So," said Hitler, "you were trying to guess your purpose here. Let's end the mystery for you."

The Führer stood and walked to the bookcase that lined the wall opposite him. He quickly found the large book he was looking for, brought it back to the conference table, and opened it to a page that had been dog-eared for easy reference.

General Kemmler looked down to see an artist's full-color rendering of the moon orbiting the Earth.

With his right hand now trembling from excitement—or possibly a chemical imbalance from the myriad of pills he self-medicated with—Hitler extended his index finger until it was touching the drawing of the moon in what Kemmler realized was a detailed book on astronomy.

"You, my General," announced Hitler, "are in the rocket business. When you look at this drawing of the moon, tell me *precisely* what you see."

Rather than try to guess the answer Hitler might be seeking, Kemmler decided to say the first things that came to his mind.

"A lifeless, airless world that controls the tides of Earth."

Hitler let out a high-pitched cackle of a laugh.

"Correct…but wrong. Wrong. Isn't that right, Martin?"

Whatever the inside joke or whatever the answer, Kemmler knew he would have to wait for the two men to play out the act.

As he looked across the table at Bormann, he noticed drool forming in the corner of the flunky's mouth.

So as not to witness it spill out onto the table, Kemmler shifted his eyes back to the drawing of the moon and awaited clarification from Hitler.

The Führer once again extended his shaking finger until it was touching the drawing.

"What you are seeing," Hitler declared, "is the answer and… the future. The *ultimate* insurance policy. A solution relayed to me from Heaven during a recent séance with my chief astrologer. You, my gifted general and rocket man, must now quickly figure out the logistics needed to project our pure Aryan seeds deep within the soil of that lifeless world, and well out of the reach of the baying half-breeds who might eventually slip through our defenses."

# 3

Eighteen months and a few days after that fateful meeting, General Kemmler looked out upon the shadowy silhouettes of ten massive rockets.

The largest and most advanced the world had *never* known. Each designed by a twenty-six-year-old protégé of chief scientist Wernher von Braun.

A young and unknown scientist by the name of Carl Oberth, who even von Braun acknowledged had the greatest mind for rocketry that he had ever encountered.

Days after von Braun had grudgingly admitted that fact, General Kemmler secretly invited the young scientist to his home on the Peenemünde base for a very private dinner.

Over the course of the dinner, the general explained exactly what was on his mind. As he did, the Oberth's eyes at first narrowed with incredulity and doubt. But as Kemmler continued to outline the plan—and the explicit orders of the Führer—the young man suddenly took a small notebook and pencil out of his inside coat pocket and furiously began to draw shapes, write mathematical equations, and list timelines.

Even though General Kemmler was still talking to him, the bespectacled scientist now heard nothing. So engrossed was he in what he recognized to not only be the greatest challenge of his life but a chance to make his ultimate dream a reality that the voice of his superior faded into annoying white noise.

The general stopped talking midsentence when he realized he had lost his audience of one to a cloud of thoughts, theories, and equations. The general stood and shook his head in amazement as he watched the young genius fill and flip previously blank pages with a speed he could not have imagined.

As he strolled to the kitchen to get them both a cup of coffee, Oberth began mumbling and talking to himself out loud as he continued to scribble.

General Kemmler was able to make out only snippets of words and phrases: "Tsiolkovsky rocket equation…Earth-moon gravitational well…direct ascent…curved trajectory…thirty-six hours…strap-on fuel tanks…minimum weight…no heat shields… no return fuel needed…no redundancy…crash land…strontium-90…thermocouples…heat sinks…electricity…five-year operational life…South Pole…water source…solar energy…"

Kemmler returned and placed the steaming cup of coffee before the scientist. Thirty minutes later, it still sat there untouched—the scientist had never even lifted his head from his nonstop computations and notes.

Finally, Oberth lifted his head, took a long sip of the now cold coffee, and looked over at the general.

"I accept your challenge," he said with a smile.

The general slowly stood to his imposing full height and looked down at the still smiling scientist with absolutely no warmth at all on his face.

"It is not a challenge, Carl," he corrected. "It is a *direct order* from the Führer. A direct order that must and *will* be kept secret from your family and colleagues."

With that made clear, he walked over to the front door of his luxurious cottage and opened it.

Two men even larger than himself with thick hairlines starting in the middle of their foreheads, and wearing long black leather trench coats, entered the home and silently nodded to the general as they walked past.

Seeing the two men, the young scientist jumped up from the chair. His eyes immediately went wide, and his face drained of all color. Such was the instant fear instilled by officers of Hitler's Gestapo.

The two human slabs of steel stopped three feet from Oberth and looked down upon his now trembling figure.

General Kemmler slowly closed his front door, walked back to his chair, took a seat, and motioned the scientist to do the same.

Oberth would have missed the chair completely and fallen to the floor had not one of the Gestapo agents noticed and violently shoved him back in line.

"Carl," began the general in a genuinely caring voice. "I don't have to explain to you who these two gentlemen are or the organization they represent. They are here to impress upon you the urgency and critical need for success of the task now before you."

Oberth barely lifted his head. As he did, his eyes focused on the highly polished black jackboots of the Gestapo agent closest to him.

"I don't need that impressed upon me. I *want* to make this happen. I…*need* to make this happen. To be involved is a dream come true. I want to volunteer to go. You will need me *if…*"

The agent closest to him reached down with lightning speed, grabbed him by the hair, and backhanded him across the face and out of the chair.

The general walked over and picked the now profusely bleeding young scientist off the floor and placed him back on his chair.

"*When* this is successful," stressed the general. "I am sure, Carl, that you meant to say '*when* this is successful.' And I am so very happy to hear you say all of that. Of course, with you saying that, and volunteering, means you are going to be devoting every waking hour of your life to this project. Every waking hour. Sadly, that will mean no more time with your young wife and two-year-old son."

The scientist sat bolt upright with the mention of them, but just as quickly recoiled back against the chair when the second agent instantly advanced upon him.

"Not to worry, Carl," said the general in a less-than-assuring voice. "While you work tirelessly here to make the Führer's dream come true, these men and their colleagues in the Gestapo will take your wife and son under their special care and protection."

"She's got a great ass," said the first Gestapo agent with a lecherous smile spreading across his scarred face.

In a blind rage, the young scientist tried to launch himself out of the chair at the agent. It was the last thing he remembered doing until waking in an infirmary bed many hours later.

# 4

General Kemmler looked down at his watch. Three minutes to the first launch.

They had pulled off the greatest technological achievement in the history of the human race. An achievement the world would never know.

Could *never* know.

The young genius Carl Oberth and his handpicked team actually did it.

Or, more accurately, *believed* they did it.

The real truth would be revealed three minutes from now, and then over the course of the next thirty-six hours.

Oberth himself was now part of the crew on one of the rockets. Because of his knowledge and gifts, he was considered an essential piece of the puzzle.

Because it in fact worked into the greater master plan, Kemmler had even allowed him to bring his wife and young son.

The general had heard rumors of just how physically appealing certain Gestapo agents found the young Mrs. Oberth, but he chose neither to confirm them nor prove them false.

It was a small price for the Oberths to pay for the greater good of the Fatherland.

Besides the young scientist and his family, each of the ten rockets carried precisely thirty passengers.

Each passenger manifest *exactly* duplicated the other.

Redundancy in skill sets was everything.

Each rocket carried identical equipment, cargo, supplies, blueprints, and building materials.

Of the thirty passengers per rocket, two were high-performance test pilots in charge of the spacecraft.

Twelve of the thirty were Hitler Youth between the ages of fifteen and eighteen. All highly athletic, all highly intelligent, all extremely virile, and *all* fanatical believers in the master race. Their first job would be to breed.

Two others were Gestapo assassins personally ordered by Hitler to eliminate anyone who showed even a hint of doubt or resistance.

The remaining passengers in each rocket were other adults. But none over the age of forty. Their number was comprised of physicians, geologists, agronomists, civil engineers, mining engineers, architects, and rocket and automotive experts. All were soldiers, and most cross-trained in at least two other specialties.

* * *

ONE HOUR BEFORE the launch, General Kemmler had ordered every single person left on the base into the confines of the massive blockhouse. This included the soldiers as well as the cooks, valets, and secretarial staff. Everyone.

There was not one human being left outside of the blockhouse.

All had also been instructed to place all of their identification and base badges into a large metal barrel just outside the door to the blockhouse.

Inside at the back of the blockhouse, they found beer, wine, water, and a full, mouthwatering buffet of food. Truly the best that money could buy.

As all of the base staff mingled around the food and alcohol stations at the back, and the soft, calming notes of a waltz played on a phonograph, Kemmler took one more look at his watch.

Two minutes to go.

He nodded to his most trusted aide, who was standing just outside the door.

The aide instantly poured a jerry can full of gasoline into the barrel holding all the staff identification, then lit a flare and dropped it in the barrel. As the flames jumped up above his head, he stepped into the blockhouse and slammed the one-foot-thick metal door shut.

Once closed, he locked it from the inside with a massive padlock and then dropped the key down a floor drain just to the left of the door.

Once done, he looked at General Kemmler, nodded his head once, saluted, and walked to the back of the room to grab a beer.

Off to the general's left, one of the three rocket technicians at the control panel began the ten-second countdown. When he reached zero, it was as if Hell on Earth had been birthed two miles from their location.

No earthquake, the general thought, could feel as violent as what began to happen.

Even through the darkness and mist of the night, the light from rocket engines was almost blinding.

Nine more times, the technician at the control panel gave the same ten-second countdown.

As the last of the rockets thundered up into the sky and beyond, General Kemmler turned to look at the men, women, and even a few children standing in awe in the back of the blockhouse. Most were holding either a drink in their hands, a plate of food, or both.

The general smiled at them, then slowly nodded.

He then turned to his right, walked three feet to stand before a lever that had only been installed days earlier, closed his eyes, and pulled it down.

No sooner did he complete that action than twenty large cyanide-filled glass bottles dropped from the ceiling and smashed onto the concrete floor of the blockhouse.

*The Russian soldiers, one or two days away at the most, would never be able to torture us to learn the deepest secret in Nazi history,* thought the general as he quickly moved to stand back in front of the small glass window of the blockhouse.

As he watched the receding flames of the tenth rocket head out of the Earth's atmosphere, he was able to draw two more breaths before the cyanide gas killed him.

# 5

At approximately seven miles altitude above the Peenemünde launch facility, each of the ten rockets entered into what is known in the aerospace world as "Max-Q."

The point where the airframe undergoes maximum and often violent mechanical stress.

Two of the ten rockets began to disintegrate from the massive turbulence before their fuel tanks exploded.

Twisted metal debris along with the body parts of the sixty passengers from the two rockets rained down upon the blackish churning waves of the Baltic Sea.

What didn't sink to the bottom miles below was quickly devoured by the predators of the deep.

Thanks to their experimental and powerful strap-on boosters, the remaining eight rockets made it out of the Earth's atmosphere on their direct ascent trajectory toward the moon. If all went as planned, the direct ascent journey from the surface of the Earth to the surface of the moon would take approximately thirty-six hours.

But nothing ever went as planned. Not in space.

Especially when you were launching untested, experimental rockets stripped down to the bare minimum to reduce launch weight.

At a height of eighty-seven miles, the main engine of rocket number 3 failed.

As it and its thirty passengers slowly fell back toward Earth and a fiery cremation in the atmosphere, the seven remaining rockets motored on in a relatively straight line to intercept the moving moon 240,000 miles away.

The young rocket scientist Carl Oberth and his team were exceptional at orbital mechanics and design. Exceptional. But even the best can't be perfect when confronting continual unknowns.

In theory, it was the simplest of mathematical equations to get from point A on the Earth to point B on the moon. Especially when one was using a direct ascent trajectory.

Unfortunately for Oberth and his fellow history-making travelers as the first humans in space, "in theory" meant less than nothing to the vacuum of space and the million ways to die that it harbored in the darkest of shadows.

Get something—anything—wrong by 1/1000th of a degree in the vacuum of space, and pay the ultimate price.

The main engine on rocket number 7 began to sputter and fire inconsistently. It quickly lost proper attitude in respect to its lunar target.

A target it would now miss thirty hours later by thousands of miles as it fell into a permanent orbit around the sun. The thirty men, women, and children on board had about seventy-two hours to enjoy the spectacular view of the passing moon and slightly approaching sun before their oxygen ran out.

Rockets 2 and 9 encountered a different problem with the same fate awaiting their passengers. The main engine of both rockets fired for seconds too long, causing them to miss their target. Condemning them to become lifeless artificial satellites orbiting the sun.

Just a few hours into the most top-secret mission in the history of the Third Reich—and the very world—and sixty passengers had been blown to bits, thirty had been burned alive, and ninety were given a two- to three-day life span before their last breaths were drawn in desperate and crazed panic.

For the four remaining rockets, Carl Oberth's orbital mechanic calculations and hardware worked to perfection.

Four of the ten rockets with their 120 surviving passengers in total now fell toward the moon and their rendezvous with destiny.

# 6

Time. *Time* was the enemy now.

For the 120 Nazis who survived the controlled crash landing on the South Pole of the moon, the clock was now ticking on their extinction.

Find a cavern inside that mountain and get to work adapting it, or perish within a few days at best.

No one needed any more motivation than that.

In the most rudimentary space suits that at least temporarily protected them against the extreme temperatures of the moon, eight geologists, eight professional miners, two civil engineers, and the officer in charge began the quarter-mile walk to the foot of the mountain.

The fact that the four remaining spaceships crash-landed so close to the mountain was no coincidence or lucky break.

As they rapidly approached the moon, the eight pilots of the four rockets had collectively agreed it was all or nothing. "We can't risk a walk of more than a mile or so," the first pilot said. "No matter how sure those geologists are that the surface is solid, the fact is, they and we *don't* know. Better to land as close to that mountain as possible or slam into it trying."

What *was* a lucky break was that as the rockets decelerated in their turn toward the South Pole of the moon, the lead pilots spotted what looked like a two-mile-long, two-hundred-yard-wide boulder-free stretch of relatively flat lunar soil just to the left of the mountain.

It was on that stretch of land that the four Nazi spaceships crash-landed and made space history in the process.

The nineteen space suit–clad men approached the mountain pulling four large plastic carts full of various tools and equipment.

Even though they were told about it and lectured on what to expect, the reality of walking and existing in gravity one-sixth of that on the Earth was a skill set that could *only* be learned from the experience of doing it.

After multiple falls and miscalculations, the nineteen got the hang of it, to varying degrees.

Two of the younger and very athletic miners became so good at it that each was "kangaroo hopping" thirty feet at a time and laughing with each vault until a sharp rebuke from their commander sounded in their headphones.

The commander also was the most experienced test pilot and senior military officer. He had zero patience for any fun or distractions. Any minutes or even seconds wasted could spell their doom.

The geologists had to find an opening in that mountain as fast as humanly possible, and then the miners had to expand it and hope it extended far enough back to accommodate them all. If not, they would use controlled explosions to make the room needed.

But first, a promising opening had to be located.

Their only need at the moment was to get *within* the moon. To place the thickest of rock walls around their bodies to protect them from the radiation and relentless dangers all about the lunar surface.

The Nazi geologists—who were in fact some of the best back on Earth—had lobbied nonstop to land on the South Pole of the moon. They felt certain it was the most compelling and inviting region on the ever-hostile world.

First and foremost, they believed the permanently shadowed craters might harbor pockets or even small reservoirs of ice in their deepest sections. Ice that could not only be used for water but for eventually making fuel.

Additionally, the mountain peak they had chosen at the South Pole was exposed to the powerful rays of the sun ninety percent of the time. Meaning, solar panels could be installed to provide electricity that would supplement the fuel cells and four small nuclear generators brought on the mission.

Beyond that, they believed the mountain had been created by violent volcanic activity hundreds of millions of years before. Volcanic activity that would make the mountain much more likely to be cavernous with lava tubes, and its substance much easier to break through than standard rock.

Barely one hour into the search, their luck continued as a promising opening was found in the forbidding walls of the mountain. An opening ten feet high and four feet wide.

Two of the geologists cautiously entered with powerful flashlights and came out two minutes later with their thumbs up and smiles on their faces. The spacious cavern—one hundred feet deep, fifty feet wide, and fifteen feet high, had apparently been blown into existence millions of years before by the intense volcanic activity of the time. Activity that had long since gone dormant.

Although the lead test pilot was indeed the commander of the mission, the geologists and engineers instantly took control and began barking out orders while continuing to walk the debris-covered floor of the cavern.

Twenty more of the strongest Nazis on the four spaceships soon joined the nineteen already working in the cavern. Aside from bringing extra tools and explosives, they also brought extra oxygen tanks.

Job one was to clear all the debris and small boulders from the floor of the cavern. Once that was accomplished, they hammered and smashed any rock formations protruding from the walls or ceiling.

Next, the engineers set off several small shaped charges to remove the largest rock barriers while making the cavern much more symmetrical.

After the cloud of the last explosion settled, the engineers got the most momentous shock of their lives. Aside from destroying the targeted rock formation, it had blown a small hole in the back wall of the cavern.

One of the engineers walked to the back and shined his flashlight into the unexpected opening. After two seconds of looking, he excitedly waved his colleague over.

The other engineer peered into the hole and actually dropped his flashlight in awe at was before him—a massive lava tube at least one hundred feet high, three hundred feet wide, and so long that the end could not be seen.

That discovery was the least consequential and fateful.

When the engineer carefully stepped through the opening to retrieve his flashlight, his feet instantly went out from underneath him and his helmeted head cracked hard on the ground.

Except…it wasn't ground.

# 7

After taking a few seconds to clear his dazed mind, the engineer slowly moved his arms about to find his flashlight, which had switched off in the fall.

After his thickly gloved right hand touched it, he slowly brought it back to his body, found the switch, and turned it back on.

When he did, the answer as to why he slipped and fell was provided. He was now sitting on a glass-like sheet of...*ice*.

Ice.

As he tentatively got up on his knees, he shone the light looking for the end of the ice.

There was none. As far as the powerful beam could penetrate, the sheet of ice went on and on and on into the darkness of the beyond.

*Ice*, he thought to himself. *Real ice.*

Ice equaled water. Water equaled the life force needed to survive.

"Ice," he thought again to himself. "Ice! Ice! Ice! Ice!"

Except he was no longer thinking to himself but screaming it into his microphone for all to hear.

"Ice, ice, ice!"

Instantly, the commander and all in the area rushed over to see the discovery.

"Ice," said the commander in a whisper once he stepped back out of the opening. "Water. Life. Future."

As the promise and possibilities of that miraculous discovery flooded his mind, he just as quickly *crushed* them.

If they did not survive the next few days, the discovery would mean nothing.

"Back to work," he screamed. "Back to work. We have to seal this cavern and power it up as fast as possible. Back to work."

Immediately, the engineers and miners went back to the task at hand.

That meant first spraying every square inch of the small cavern with a thick rubberized material created by the civil engineers to coat the walls and ceiling. An off-white gunk that would make the cavern airtight and smooth to the touch.

As it was drying, metal beams and small doors specially made in a Nazi factory were brought from the spaceships. Metal beams and doors that would comprise the inner and outer doors of the airlock entrances to the quickly evolving moon base.

The first was built around the outside opening to the cavern. The next was built into the back opening that led to the massive ice cavern beyond.

Aside from the overriding joy the commander felt regarding the discovery of ice, as a military man, he was almost as equally happy to have a back door as an escape hatch should the need ever arise.

Next, multiple fuel cells were brought from the spaceships and installed. Fuel cells that would supply not only power but oxygen, and desperately needed water as well.

Nazi spies in 1940 Britain had obtained the plans for a functioning fuel cell created by Francis Thomas Bacon. Once stolen, Nazi scientists—with *only* this mission in mind—had greatly improved their efficiency as well as their water and oxygen output.

Aside from the fuel cells, Nazi scientists had also been experimenting with something called radioisotope thermoelectric generators. These generators had no moving parts and used an array of thermocouples to convert the heat released by the decay of radioactive material into electricity.

Four of them had been built and perfected. Two were now being installed hundreds of feet from the front entrance of the base, while the other two would be held in reserve.

Heavy-duty power cords were attached to the units, and then the small nuclear generators were buried under the lunar soil to shield the radiation they gave off.

Everything now happening seemed like a well-rehearsed play. It seemed that way because it *had* been rehearsed. Dozens of times back on Earth, the Nazi crews had practiced their specific duties over and over again.

Now, as they continually trooped in and out of the transforming lunar cavern single file, they looked like a small army of ants expertly excavating a new home.

For the next three days, the 120 Nazis worked in choreographed shifts of four hours at a time. The progress was remarkable.

It had to be. Their lives depended upon it.

After the cavern was rated ready for human habitation by the engineers, the Nazi moon settlers moved in food, medical supplies, radio equipment, electrical equipment, tools, repair benches, small lathes, lights, folding chairs, tables, cots, chemical toilets, solar panels, and other essential supplies.

Last to be moved was a fairly large cache of weapons and ammunition.

After the last test on the atmosphere inside the approximately five-thousand-square-foot cavern was conducted, and proved successful, all of the passengers were moved inside and the airlock sealed.

All were exhausted to the point of collapsing. Rest, water, and food were essential before the next mission could be undertaken—that being to cannibalize the rockets outside for every single piece of metal, material, and remaining equipment. No bolt, rivet, or hint of anything Earth-made would be left behind.

All would be needed to expand their new home into the massive ice cavern. One room and one success at a time.

Operation Wolf Lair was a success, and the moon was uninhabited no more.

It was a possession of the Nazi war machine.

# 8

*July 20, 1969*

The *Eagle* had indeed landed.

At 4:18 p.m. EDT, the American lunar module carrying astronauts Neil Armstrong and Buzz Aldrin landed at the Sea of Tranquility on the surface of the moon.

Approximately six and a half hours later at 10:56 p.m. EDT, Neil Armstrong made his way down the ladder of the lunar module and then ever so tentatively stepped upon the surface.

As the first human ever to set foot on the moon, he was expected to mark the historic occasion with words to match the achievement.

Five hundred million humans back on Earth were watching him live on television in eager anticipation.

Armstrong did not disappoint when the first words spoken from the lunar surface by a human being were: *"That's one small step for a man, one giant leap for mankind."*

\* \* \*

EIGHT HUNDRED YARDS AWAY, with the sun directly at their back, two space-suited Nazi astronauts lying beneath moon-colored camouflaged capes silently observed and recorded Armstrong and then his colleague Aldrin as they walked about their spacecraft for the next two and a half hours.

Three years before Armstrong and Aldrin landed on the moon, the lunar-based Nazi scientists had been able to intercept radio and television transmissions from Earth. Neither the landing nor the landing site were a surprise.

The two Nazis now looking over the ridge were stone-faced and quiet up until the moment the Americans dared to plant their flag upon the surface.

As that happened, one instantly swore. Both had pure hate and disgust pouring out of their eyes at the supreme insult playing out before them.

That flag would not be allowed to stand.

*Especially*, thought the first Nazi astronaut darkly, *considering what today represents for us.*

\* \* \*

THE TWO MUCH LARGER than normal Nazi astronauts were both Hitler Youth when they crash-landed on the moon twenty-four years earlier.

Now, they were forty-year-old men who had been taught, and deeply believed, that Adolf Hitler was a messiah sent down by God to rescue the Aryan race from the dogs of humanity bent upon its destruction.

They were two Nazi soldiers who had spent the majority of their lives on the moon. A world and a surface they now traversed regularly with the expertise of natives.

Natives who would repel *all* invaders.

"What should we do?" asked the second Nazi astronaut who was forcing himself to stay motionless and not reach for the high-powered rifle by his side adapted to lunar conditions.

"Nothing," answered the first as his arctic-blue eyes narrowed to slits. "We have our orders. They must never know we are here. *Never*. Continue to observe and film them. They will be leaving soon. And when they do, we will go over and deal with the insult they left behind on *our* world."

* * *

THE NAZI LUNAR WOLF LAIR, which housed 120 men and women twenty-four years earlier, was now the home to over 1,000.

Over one thousand now "Lunarians" who had not only pushed their home base deep into the massive lava tube, but had never forgotten the most valuable lesson of their lives. A lesson taught to them regularly on the moon and that inspired them daily.

That lesson being the Nazi war machine's brilliant circumvention of the humiliating and punitive Treaty of Versailles.

A "treaty"—as all young Nazi Lunarians were now taught in school—that ultimately gave birth to the supremacy of the Aryan race.

Almost to a person, every German alive during the signing of the treaty in the Hall of Mirrors at the Palace of Versailles in France on June 28, 1919, or born after, had believed it was excessively cruel to the German people.

Not only had resentment and the need for revenge continue to build in the minds of the German people, but so had their creative ways to get around the treaty and reestablish their war machine.

Years after the treaty was signed, even independent historians of the time believed it to be incredibly unfair to the German people, and thus a rallying cry that had helped facilitate the rise of the madman Adolf Hitler.

The Treaty of Versailles laid virtually all the blame for World War I, and its destruction and loss of life, at the feet of Germany.

As such, the Allies united as one to extract their pound of flesh from the German people. And extract it they did.

The "treaty" was really presented to the German negotiators as a *fait accompli*. One almost entirely drafted by Britain, France, and the United States with zero input from Germany.

As they were being forced to accept the guilt for the war, 10 percent of Germany was immediately taken from them and ceded to other countries. *Ten percent* of the entire country.

Because the treaty had deemed Germany the "aggressor" of the war, it stipulated that Germany and Germany alone was responsible for making reparations to the Allied nations for losses and damages they sustained during the war.

The amount owed by Germany, as spelled out in the treaty, came to $33 billion in 1921 dollars. An amount guaranteed to not only financially cripple the country for years or decades to come, but also prevent it from reconstituting its formerly very powerful military.

Or, so it was thought.

Beyond that financial price, Germany could have no more than one hundred thousand soldiers, and was forbidden to manufacture any tanks, armored cars, airplanes, submarines, or weapons larger than those needed for a token police force.

The effects of the Treaty of Versailles on the German people were devastating.

And yet, at least in the minds of many of the German people, it was *that* very "treaty" that united their spirit as *one* and allowed them, by hook and by crook, to rebuild what would turn out to be the most powerful war machine the world had ever known. All while still struggling to eat and survive.

And while the nation was indeed suffering greatly during those years, it still managed to pull off the impossible.

By 1939, the broken, beaten, defeated, and humiliated Germany had over one million soldiers, over eight thousand aircraft, and almost one hundred warships. A force built from rubble that became the hated and feared Nazi war machine.

A fact and a story that had been pounded into the heads of the Nazi children born, and now thriving, on the moon.

"The world," stressed the lunar commander over and over again to various classes at lunar school, "believes that it vanquished us. That we are no more. That we will never again be able to reconstitute our forces, our might, and our ethnic superiority and impose ourselves upon them again. But, my children, as you are being taught, they believed the exact same thing when they forced that wretched Treaty of Versailles upon us. The *exact* same thing. But look what we accomplished in the twenty years after. Look what we built. Now, look inward. Look what we have accomplished and built on this strange new world in just over twenty years! We are experts at pulling off the impossible. *Experts*. Our science is not only matching what they have back on Earth but *exceeding* it. The world believes us an evil relic of the past swept into the dustbin of its false history. But look, my children. Look out the window and see what I see. From where we sit, we can see the entire Earth. All of it. And one day, when *we* are ready, we will punish it for what it did to our ancestors and our beloved Fatherland. One day soon."

# 9

*July 20, 2029*

Sixty years to the day after Neil Armstrong and Buzz Aldrin landed on the moon, eight Chinese taikonauts in two separate landers touched down upon the lunar soil.

China had won the new space race between them, the United States, and Russia.

They did so because they were single-minded in approach.

Because the Chinese human spaceflight program was run entirely by the military, there were no illusions as to their mission to the moon—that exclusive mission being to establish the ultimate "high ground."

Period.

No matter what was stipulated in the Outer Space Treaty, the subsequent Moon Treaty, or the language signed off on by the United Nations General Assembly regarding the "Peaceful Uses of Outer Space," the Chinese taikonauts preparing to emerge from their landers were about to claim the moon as a sovereign territory of the People's Republic of China.

Sovereign territory that would be theirs forever more.

Sadly…some dreams die faster than others.

*Much* faster.

\* \* \*

SIXTY YEARS TO THE DAY since Armstrong and Aldrin had landed on the moon also meant sixty years to the day since the two Nazi astronauts lay in hiding observing and filming them.

Six decades.

Six decades for the Nazis to breed and multiply. Six decades for them to turn a moon colony into a space city. Six decades for them to scout and then inhabit other strategic locations on the moon. Six decades for them to perfect their science. Six decades for them to build an army. Six decades for them to start and then perfect a space force. Six decades for them to not only adapt to the moon, but to become one with it.

Six decades that allowed the Nazis to discover an unlimited supply of helium-3. The ideal fuel for the fusion reactors they had been operating for over ten years.

Six decades in which the Nazi leadership on the moon quickly learned that the one-sixth gravity of their new home created an amazing and much-desired side effect in their master race. That being that each new generation of children being born on the moon was growing taller. Dramatically taller. A growth rate greatly enhanced by the tremendous progress their scientists were making with regard to human genetic modification.

With that science, and without the crushing and limiting anchor of Earth's gravity, Nazi men were now growing to an average of eight feet tall, Nazi women an average of six and a half feet tall. Each succeeding generation being more genetically modified than the previous and improved for strength, speed, agility, intelligence, and life span.

The Nazi leadership now truly believed that it's master race was evolving into a "super race."

*The* super race of the solar system.

And because of this evolution, those same Nazi leaders now knew that the time had come.

*Their* time had come.

For it was *they* who in reality controlled the ultimate high ground. And had done so for years.

A high ground and a revered day now being desecrated for the second time by invaders.

To the now thousands of Nazi Lunarians, July 20 was akin to a religious holiday on Earth. It represented the day when, in 1944, a mongrel pack of impure traitorous Germans involved in Operation Valkyrie had tried to assassinate the messiah Adolf Hitler.

It was a day of true reverence to the Nazi Lunarians, because they were taught that it was the very hand of God that extended down from Heaven that day and shielded the messiah Hitler against the deadly effects of the bomb blast.

July 20 was the holiest day on their lunar calendar.

After God intervened to save him, the messiah Hitler himself said: "I regard this as a confirmation of the task imposed upon me by God. The great cause which I serve will be brought through its present perils, and everything will come to a good end."

Every Nazi on the moon was required to memorize that quote as children, and then recite it on command as adults. Something all did with immense pride.

Sixty years ago today, thought the Nazi commander, the Americans dishonored our holiest of days when their two astronauts not only set foot upon our world but planted their abhorrent flag in the surface.

We could do nothing that long-ago day. We could do nothing because we were still in the infant stage and had to remain hidden and unknown.

But now…but *now*, thought the commander with a truly malevolent smile, *we are the masters of all we see.* From the surface of the moon to the surface of the Earth. No one will dishonor our most holiest of days ever again. *Ever.*

That the leaders of the People's Republic of China had picked July 20 as the day to land on the moon *only* as a sophomoric insult to the Americans was of no consequence to the Nazi commander.

Blasphemy a second time would not be tolerated. The punishment was clear.

The painful and indeed horrifying lessons the Earth was about to be taught began now.

Today.

# 10

On televisions, computers, smartphones, and even the rare radio, much of the world was preparing to witness the Chinese taikonauts descend from their lunar landers and step foot upon the surface of the moon. They would be the first human beings to do so since Apollo 17 American astronaut Eugene Cernan left the last footprint in its dust on December 14, 1972.

But now, fifty-seven years after that last forgotten footprint was made, much of the world of 2029 was taking a somewhat perverse pleasure in seeing the Americans—the great and powerful United States...the last true remaining superpower—lose this particular space race. A race they had lost to an Asian nation. A race they had lost to a nation many in the United States still felt was "Third World" at best.

Hundreds of millions of people, from Indonesia to Latin America, felt a real sense of pride that the Chinese had beat the Americans.

The Americans, who always seemed to win everything on Earth, had lost the race back to the moon.

Again, that the People's Republic of China may have been racing to the moon only to claim it as their own and establish a military outpost with military objectives meant little or nothing to those millions of mostly poor and struggling people around the world.

The arrogant Americans had finally been beat at something truly significant, and that was good enough for them.

Before that last American had stepped back inside his lunar module to depart the moon, he made an attempt at predicting the future:

"As I take man's last step from the surface...for some time to come...I'd like to say what I believe history will record. That America's challenge of today has forged man's destiny of tomorrow. And that as we leave the moon...we leave as we came, and God willing, as we shall return. With peace and hope for all mankind."

A prediction those who landed on the moon in secret twenty-seven years *before* those quixotic and short-sighted words were spoken were about to bury deep within the lunar surface, where it could properly and deservedly decompose.

* * *

As could be predicted, the military leaders of the Chinese space program did not allow the live cameras to be turned on until it was clear their two spacecraft had landed safely on the moon and all was well with the crew.

By the time the live feed was allowed to be shown to all on Earth, the eight taikonauts were already out of their landers and walking tentatively about the surface.

Not believing in wasting time or uttering foolish "historic" words of no consequence from the moon, the commander of the Chinese taikonauts stood before the main camera on the surface, raised the gold visor of his space helmet, and began to address the almost one billion people on Earth watching his every move:

*"To all those on Earth, we are here to proclaim, that from this day forth, the moon and all of its mineral wealth is a territory of the People's Republic of China and will be thought of and protected as such. We further proclaim..."*

At that exact second, all communication with the eight taikonauts on the lunar surface, as well as the two orbiting the moon in the carrier ship that would bring them and four of the eight taikonauts on the surface back to Earth, was lost.

More than that, all telemetry whatsoever was cut off.

As the Chinese army colonel who was the commander of this historic mission looked at his fellow taikonauts in mild confusion, he saw something crest over the horizon that made his blood run cold.

It looked for all the world like a giant two-toned lunar spider. Most of it all black, with the very top in the camouflaged colors of the lunar surface.

That it was something mechanical, he had no doubt.

The Chinese military commander pressed a button on his space-suited right forearm to speak to his fellow taikonauts and quickly learned that even the communication between them had been cut off. They were, for all intents and purposes, each individually deaf.

As the seven other taikonauts saw the panic reflected in their commander's eyes, they turned their heads to discover its source.

Except when they did, another one of these massive lunar spiders broke the horizon. And then another. All equidistant from the other and surrounding the two Chinese landers.

As the other taikonauts now gathered around him, the commander wondered if it was some strange hallucination, a mirage one sees on the deserts of the Earth, or even some twisted test set up by the leadership of China to test their courage and resolve.

Obviously, this could not be real.

# 11

The "imaginary" lunar spiders were about to prove themselves all too real. Because of their black color and the two oval windows up front—which did, to the Chinese commander, resemble glowing yellow eyes—the squat, wide, thirty-foot-long eight-wheeled vehicles truly did seem like some hulking alien arachnid preparing to pounce on their prey.

After an agonizingly long five minutes, a hatch opened in each of the three vehicles. From each hatch, a being in a space suit stepped out. Then another. And another.

At the sight of them, a male officer to the left of the Chinese commander fainted in terror.

Each of the creatures that stepped out of the vehicles was at least eight feet tall. And each was carrying some kind of powerful-looking weapon in their hands.

Within two minutes, twenty-four of these massive beings in black space suits, black helmets, and black-tinted visors emerged from the three vehicles.

One of the beings—the Chinese commander guessed the leader—was standing several feet in front of the others.

In his right hand, he held one of those powerful-looking weapons. In his left hand, he seemed to be holding a small remote control.

With the thumb of his gloved left hand, he pushed a button on the remote control. One second after he did, the terrifyingly impossible was revealed.

Just below the habitation cabins of each lunar spider, a self-lit, six-foot-diameter circular panel flashed open to showcase the Nazi swastika in all of its black, red, and white glory.

The Chinese commander's jaw literally dropped open, and his mind went blank at the macabre scene playing out before him.

As the other six still-standing taikonauts—comprised of four male and two female military personnel—inched even closer to their commander, the twenty-four space-suited creatures began advancing toward them in graceful, clearly well-practiced giant leaps. Each leap reached an apex of twenty feet while covering at least forty feet of lunar soil.

When they landed from their last jump just ten feet in front of them, the Chinese commander literally felt the ground shake beneath his boots. Each of the creatures had to be at least three hundred Earth pounds.

As they landed in a perfect semicircle around the taikonauts, the beings pulled a lever on their weapons and then aimed them at the Chinese.

The leader of the beings slowly walked up to the now trembling taikonauts, lifted his black-tinted visor, and looked down upon the one he guessed to be their commander.

The Chinese colonel was a good six feet tall. Even at that, he stood in amazement as he looked up another two-plus feet into the face of…a monster.

It was a human face, but the comparison stopped there.

The head and face looked as if they were carved out of granite. Flesh-covered granite. But it was the eyes that most captivated the attention of the Chinese commander. Eyes that were unnaturally blue and all but alien to him. But not quite. The Chinese commander had encountered eyes like those once before in his lifetime. It was while scuba diving off the coast of Nicaragua. One second he was alone twenty feet underwater with his thoughts; the next, a great white shark bumped him from behind. As he turned in fright to face it, he was staring directly into one of the eyes of the great white. An eye that seemed dead of any emotion. Any emotion minus the merciless task at hand. To kill and devour its prey.

In the creature now before him, the colonel saw those same dead eyes. As he looked into their unblinking stare, he knew, beyond a shadow of a doubt, that the great white was no match for the evil now personified before him.

Without saying a word, the lead creature looked at the being to his immediate right and nodded down at the taikonaut who had passed out.

The giant lunar being nodded back, walked over to the prone figure, and, with one hand, lifted him like he was nothing more than a rag doll and threw his body one hundred feet to the left, where it crashed into a boulder.

The lead being then looked down at the others, pointed at the taikonaut one hundred feet away, and motioned them to move next to his body.

Once the taikonauts were all gathered around their fallen comrade, two of the beings seemed to appear out of nowhere. One holding four shovels. The other three.

With his massive right boot, the lead being made an outline in the lunar soil about thirty feet long and four feet wide.

Then, with an easily understood gesture, he instructed the taikonauts to dig.

As the seven taikonauts dug, eight of the twenty-four beings leaped over to the two Chinese lunar landers and began to methodically take apart the control cabins and bring the pieces collected to huge storage units on the back of the lunar spiders.

After thirty minutes, the lead being motioned for the digging to stop. He nodded again at the one who seemed to be his second in command. That impossibly imposing figure nodded back, walked over and picked up the clearly dead taikonaut he had thrown against the rock, and deposited the now lifeless corpse in the bottom of the ditch.

Once done, he jerked the shovels out of the hands of the mentally numb taikonauts.

All mentally numb except the Chinese commander. He took one quick look into the dead ice-blue eyes of the lead creature, nodded his head in silent acknowledgment, then turned and focused his eyes on the planet Earth rising just above the horizon.

Home.

He then closed his eyes, smiled to himself, and thought of his family.

\* \* \*

The fleetingly false dream of Chinese domination of the moon ended that second.

The seven remaining taikonauts never moved again of their own volition. Without one word ever being spoken, four of the lunar beings stepped forward and pulled the triggers of their weapons.

High-velocity projectiles instantly and silently ripped into and through the five men and two women. One second they stood on the surface, the next they were flung above it. Multiple streams of crimson red mist leapt from each of them as the projectiles exited their bodies. Before the seven could settle back to the surface, the natural gases within those now shredded bodies exploded when exposed to the violent vacuum of space. As those fluids boiled and the gases hissed, the bodies continued their grotesque dance about the surface of the moon.

Finally, they came to rest. Three had fallen into the ditch they helped dig while the other four were kicked into it by two of the beings.

Once the last of the eight was in, the ditch was filled back in with lunar soil and smoothed over.

That task quickly completed, the lead creature coldly turned his head to observe the dismantling of the Chinese control cabins.

As the Nazis had done since the first unmanned spacecraft successfully landed on the moon in the late 1950s, they would take every last bit of the technology. Learn from it. Copy it. And then… improve upon it.

# 12

As the three Nazi lunar spiders were returning back to the Wolf Lair—each one pulling a specially designed weighted mesh to not only cover their tracks but return the soil to its natural look—a much more critically important military operation was taking place seventy miles above them in lunar orbit.

Much like their now dead and buried colleagues on the moon, the two remaining taikonauts in the Chinese carrier rocket were completely cut off from the Earth.

Worse, along with losing all of their communication connections, everything else—including their life support and oxygen systems—had ceased to function at the exact same instant.

Sitting in the now darkness of their cabin only illuminated from the reflected light of the lunar surface filtering in through two small windows, the taikonauts did not have to be told what to do.

It was either get into the space suits immediately and be afforded a few more hours of oxygen, or die from a combination of carbon monoxide and rapidly dwindling breathable air in their cabin.

Three minutes after getting into their space suits, something remarkably curious happened.

Two relatively small and extremely sleek all-black spacecraft eased into position on either side of the Chinese carrier rocket.

As one of the taikonauts noticed the movement in the window out of the corner of his eye, he floated over to have a better look.

What he saw filled his mind with even more confusion.

The taikonaut had long been a student of aviation and space history. Back on Earth, his computer was filled with hundreds of files on the subjects.

What he was now seeing was right out of one of those files, except…that was impossible.

The spacecraft outside his window looked very much like the X-20 Dyna-Soar conceived by Boeing for the American space program.

The X-20 was an incredibly practical "space plane" capable of carrying out a variety of military missions, including aerial and space reconnaissance, bombing runs, space interception and fighting, and the capture or sabotage of enemy satellites.

Even though it was a true spacecraft, it could land on a runway on Earth if needed and be used multiple times.

As far as the taikonaut was concerned, it was *the* most amazing spacecraft *never* built, having been cancelled in 1963 right before initial production.

And yet, there outside his window in a parking orbit was almost an exact duplicate of the dual-finned, sleek black killing machine.

"Impossible," the taikonaut said out loud.

As he spoke the word, his comrade began to vigorously shake his shoulder after noticing the twin spacecraft on the other side.

"We are saved," he mouthed through the faceplate of his helmet. "We are saved. The Americans or the Russians are outside our window. I don't know how and I don't care at the moment. We are saved."

The first taikonaut suddenly felt a wave of foreboding wash over him. Whoever or whatever was outside their windows, he felt for certain it wasn't the Americans or the Russians.

As that thought filled his mind, the other taikonaut shook him again.

"The hatch. They are opening the hatch to their spacecraft."

The first taikonaut slowly floated over to look out the window. By the time he got situated, there was already some kind of astronaut in an all-black space suit floating outside and seemingly waving them over.

"It *is* a rescue," declared the second taikonaut. "We are saved."

The first sat back from the window and shook his head. Something was wrong. They must not step outside. Of that, he was certain.

Too late.

His comrade was already manually opening their own hatch.

"Wait," yelled the first taikonaut as he propelled himself across the cabin to stop the process.

The second taikonaut was motivated by an unassailable fact. The oxygen in their space suits was quickly running out and when gone, they would die of asphyxiation. End of story.

For that simple reason, he pushed his panicked colleague away and finished manually opening the door to the vacuum of space.

When fully opened, he was met with yet another surreal sight.

That of the face of the most beautiful woman he had ever seen in his life. A face framed perfectly behind the faceplate of her space helmet.

The taikonaut imagined that, as they were in space and therefore maybe closer to Heaven, this was the face of a true angel. Bright blue eyes, perfect skin, a shock of blonde hair resting upon her forehead. All lit up by the warmest and most welcoming smile he had ever witnessed.

He waved frantically for his comrade to join him at the open hatch.

The first taikonaut, realizing both his train of thought and position were ultimately untenable, reluctantly drifted over to the hatch.

The female astronaut, clearly tethered to her two-person spacecraft, was now just two meters from them. Like his comrade—who had already pushed himself out toward her welcoming arms—he had never seen such beauty in a woman before.

Literally breathtakingly beautiful, in fact.

Just as his comrade reached her, she instantly pulled a twelve-inch-long military-grade bayonet from her black space suit and plunged it all the way to the hilt into the torso of the taikonaut.

With unimaginable speed, she shoved the dying taikonaut away from her and advanced on the second.

He had incredibly quick reflexes, but not nearly quick enough.

He instantly pushed himself off his own spacecraft and began to float away. As he did, the angel's smiling face was suddenly above his for just a second before switching to a look of disgust reserved for a lesser species one was about to put out of its misery under the heel of a shoe.

With her smile back in place, he caught a reflection of light off the steel of the bayonet as she moved it toward him. Surprisingly to him, she did not plunge it into him. Rather, she simply cut his oxygen line and pushed him farther away from the spacecraft.

For some reason—maybe the need to live one or two minutes longer—he drew in a deep breath and held it.

As he floated away from the spacecraft at a steady two miles per hour, he noticed a second—much larger—black space-suited figure exit their equally black and sleek-looking spacecraft.

With his lungs now screaming for air, he let out his breath and breathed in…nothing.

Just as life was leaving him, the taikonaut saw the two black space-suited figures maneuvering a fairly large black cylinder into the carrier rocket.

"Strange," was the last word his mind ever formed.

# 13

The People's Republic of China did beat the United States to the moon. But only by less than a day.

While it was indeed a race for prestige, pride, and especially territory, the United States would never admit as such.

Much like the Nazi geologists eighty-four years earlier, the Americans chose to land near the South Pole of the moon for the incredible promise it held in sustaining future missions and a planned moon base.

Life is nothing if not ironic, with just a smidge of poetic justice sprinkled on top.

Completely oblivious as to what had happened on the lunar surface eighty-four years ago, as well as the fate that befell the Chinese taikonauts just hours before, the occupants of the three-person American lander made a perfect four-point landing on the moon just twenty miles from the entrance to the Wolf Lair.

Unlike the secretive Chinese, the Americans were only too happy to broadcast every single second of the landing.

With multiple mini-HD cameras situated around the bottom of the lander pointing in every direction, the successful landing proved to be wonderful and even captivating viewing.

Except, unlike the almost one billion people on Earth tuning in to watch the Chinese taikonauts on the moon, this event was watched by only about three hundred million.

A very large number indeed, but still a drop off of almost seven hundred million from the Chinese landing—the main reason again being a worldwide tiredness regarding the Americans and whatever "first" they were about to once again claim.

Regardless of their actual motivations and growing muscular power, the People's Republic of China and its taikonauts were still viewed as the "underdog."

People loved to cheer for the underdog.

The three-person crew in the American lander could not care less about the latest space race, the underdogs who claimed the largest viewing audience, or any of the geopolitical bullshit that might be playing out back on Earth.

They cared only about landing their spacecraft safely, conducting a very successful one-week surface exploratory mission aboard the lunar rover they carried, and then blasting off to dock with their fellow astronaut in lunar orbit, rocketing out of orbit, and getting their asses back to Earth.

Each of the three astronauts aboard the lander was picked precisely because they were highly qualified, no nonsense, off-the-charts intelligent, and incredibly goal oriented.

The commander of the mission was thirty-two-year-old US Air Force Major Ian Stewart. Though born in Boston, a large part of him had always felt Canadian as well. His great-grandfather had emigrated from Sydney, Nova Scotia, to Boston in search of work and settled there after meeting the love of his life, Anna.

While Stewart was now a third-generation American, he still had more relatives in Canada than the US, and visited them often when exploring his second home country.

Both of his parents became educators and accepted teaching positions at Boston College. Soon after that, his parents bought a house in Westwood in the hopes of affording Stewart and his little sister the best quality of life possible.

Fifteen years later, after finishing first in his class at Westwood High School, it was expected by all in the family that he would go on to Boston College and then graduate school beyond that.

At seventeen years of age, Stewart shocked them all by announcing that—on his own—he had not only completed all the steps necessary to apply to the United States Air Force Academy but had indeed been accepted.

While his parents would have preferred that he listed a truly lofty reason for his sudden interest in the Air Force Academy, and all things space, the actual truth was it had been triggered when he saw the very first *Guardians of the Galaxy* movie back in 2014.

That comedic space opera somehow created an insatiable desire to learn everything human spaceflight related.

While excelling at the Air Force Academy, and reading everything he could lay his hands on or download regarding the X-15 program, Project Mercury, Project Gemini, the Apollo program, the Space Shuttle program, Orion, and the various private sector entrants into the human spaceflight arena, it was announced that the United States was redirecting its human spaceflight program back to the moon.

Bingo. "Star Lord" now had a fixed goal and destination.

As with Westwood High, Stewart graduated at the top of his class from the Air Force Academy.

Beyond his mind, Stewart believed it crucial to keep his six-foot, four-inch 210-pound body in the best shape possible.

Aside from personal workouts in the gym, he spent four years as a tight end for the football team at the academy, as well as running track in the spring. Physical excellence that would be seen as a huge plus for his chosen career field.

As graduation approached, he was convinced the quickest career path to him becoming a NASA astronaut was to become, first, a high-performance jet pilot, and from there move on to test pilot.

One month into training to fly the Lockheed Martin–built F-35 Lightning fighter jet, he sent his application to NASA. It was rejected.

The next time he applied, he had over two thousand hours in high-performance jets and a growing reputation for being an all-around prodigy. Someone who was exceptional at everything simply because it was in him to be so.

He made the next NASA selection process and redirected every bit of his intelligence, skill, and passion toward being on the first lunar landing mission since Apollo 17.

\* \* \*

Venus Washington never wanted to become a pilot, but she did love cracking open rocks.

Back in the day, her mom Barbara had played tennis at Howard University and then continued to follow the sport after graduation. Like many women of color—then and since—she took particular pride in the accomplishments of Venus and Serena Williams.

Toward the end of the year 2000, and right around the time her first child and daughter was about to be born, Venus Williams went on a tennis winning streak that captivated the entire sporting world. She not only won thirty-five matches in a row—including six tournaments—but also won Olympic Gold in singles and doubles as well as winning her first two majors.

After witnessing most of that historic streak, Barbara knew that "Venus" was the only name possible for her precious little baby girl.

Like her mom, Venus Washington went to Howard University. Unlike her mom, who majored in philosophy, Venus attended the Department of Physics and Astronomy majoring in physics. In the summer between her junior and senior year, she took a cross-country trip with her cousin, with the final destination being her cousin's home in Los Angeles. Along the way, they stopped in Hutchinson, Kansas, where Venus stumbled upon a tour of the Kansas Underground Salt Museum. At 650 feet beneath the surface, as she looked at the rocks and tried to divine the mysteries within them, she became hooked on geology.

After graduating with her degree in physics from Howard, she applied to and was accepted by Stanford, where she got her PhD in geological sciences.

Right before graduation, she saw a small article in her college paper stating that NASA was looking for geologists to become astronauts.

Like Ian Stewart, she had also heard or read somewhere that NASA was going to be sending humans back to the moon.

The *moon*.

Talk about a geologist's dream come true.

Venus applied and was accepted to the next astronaut class.

Also like Ian Stewart, the five-foot, ten-inch Venus Washington was a big believer in staying in the best shape possible. While at Howard she'd matched her mom by playing for the tennis team. Once out in the much warmer weather of California, Washington started to participate in monthly mini-triathlon competitions.

Aside from the physical benefits, Washington did it because it helped to decompress her continually cluttered mind.

\* \* \*

ROBERT MARSHALL—THE THIRD MEMBER of the crew—was in anything but great shape. At forty-seven years of age, the five-foot, eight-inch MIT grad and computer and mechanical genius had a bit of a potbelly offset by a "please don't notice" comb-over hairstyle and pasty-white skin that had clearly not sat under the vitamin D–producing rays of the sun for years.

NASA couldn't care less what he looked like, or his aversion to physical and outdoor activity. He was by far the most qualified person on the planet Earth at not only understanding the mechanics and software needed to run the lunar lander and lunar rover, but also knowing how to diagnose and repair any problem if needed.

As Marshall was fond of saying back in Houston, "If I can't fix it, it ain't broke."

# 14

"Say again, Houston," asked Stewart just after he, Washington, and Marshall had climbed into their space suits in preparation for their initial EVA on the surface of the moon.

The first Americans to do so since Eugene Cernan stepped off the surface fifty-seven years earlier.

"Just wanted to triple-check that all systems in the lander are operating as normal and the communication signal is strong, *over*."

The thick-brown-haired Stewart squinted his gray eyes as he looked over at Washington and Marshall. Both shrugged their shoulders as they did a final check on their suits.

"Roger that, Houston," confirmed Stewart. "Everything here is nominal, green, and working like a charm."

"Roger that, Ian. We are very happy to hear that down here."

Stewart now frowned as he looked again at his colleagues. This was the fourth time in the last few hours Houston had sounded a bit strange...even mysterious.

While still in lunar orbit and just before they descended to the lunar surface, Stewart, Washington, and Marshall had been told of the complete loss of signal from both the taikonauts on the surface as well as from their carrier rocket in orbit.

The immediate assumption from Houston and others was either a breakdown in the Chinese technology or possibly some kind of solar flare.

But if it was a solar flare, thought Stewart at the time, wouldn't they have lost all communications as well?

"Roger, Houston," replied Stewart in a now more serious tone. "Is there anything else we need to know? Venus already has her geology hammer out and is champing at the bit to get out and start cracking open some moon rocks. If I don't let her out now, she may use the hammer on the hatch."

"Roger that, Ian," laughed the CapCom back at his station in Houston. "All good. NSA is reporting to us that the Chinese are going bat-shit trying to figure out what happened and reestablish conta—"

At that precise second, all communication with both the American lander and carrier rocket in orbit was lost. In addition, every system for both spacecraft also shut down. Life support included.

As Stewart, Washington, and Marshall were locking their helmets into place and activating the life-support system in their suits, Ian saw a shadow creep across a sunlit strip of lunar soil visible just outside the port window.

With his helmet now locked in place and oxygen flowing through the suit, he stepped over to the window and looked out.

Not more than thirty feet from the lander, a massive spider-like vehicle had come to rest. As he tried to wrap his mind around what was happening before him, the hatch on the habitation module opened and something large, menacing, and clearly humanoid began to step out.

As he turned toward Washington and Marshall in distressed confusion, he noticed the six-foot-wide symbol on the front of the vehicle.

After the split second it took his mind to comprehend what he was looking at, his left knee buckled in reaction. Washington reached out in a flash to steady him as she craned her neck to see what caused such a spell.

# 15

Ian Stewart stared in stunned disbelief at the Nazi swastika glowing in red, black, and white on the front of the massive wheeled vehicle.

As his mind began to click back into place, he looked on in even more horror at the impossibly large humanoids exiting the vehicle and beginning to fan out around their lunar lander. Each one at least eight feet in height and twice as wide as a man on Earth.

And each one, clearly carrying some kind of weapon.

"There is no way we are seeing this," said Washington as she craned her neck around Stewart to look out the window.

"Seeing what?" asked Marshall as he tried to look between his much taller colleagues.

Stewart stepped out of the way to give Marshall an unimpeded view.

"Holy shit," yelled Marshall. "Holy fuck. Holy shit. What the fu…. This has to be some kind of twisted joke, right? I mean… what the fuck?"

Stewart stepped back in front of the window and watched as one of the immense beings in an all-black space suit walked closer to their lander.

"I don't think it's any kind of joke," said Stewart in a calm but resigned voice. "And joke or not, it does not matter one bit. Our lander has lost all power and life support. Obviously, whoever or whatever those things are out there are responsible for that. We have a few hours of oxygen left in our suits. So…"

Before he could continue, Washington spoke out in a nervous whisper.

"That giant thing is motioning for us to come out."

Stewart looked down to see the being in black calmly waving them out. He then pointed at his wrist to an imaginary watch and held up his hand to indicate "five minutes."

As soon as he did, Stewart could see the being's lips move through his tinted visor and suddenly, two more of the beings walked up next to him and pointed their lethal-looking weapons up at the window they stood behind.

"Time to go meet the new neighbors," said Stewart with a slight chuckle.

"What?!" yelled Marshall. "You can't be fuckin' serious."

"He's right, Robert," said Washington before Stewart could answer. "What's our only alternative? Sit in here and die from asphyxiation when our suit oxygen runs out."

"I've got news for you," interjected Stewart with a much more commanding voice. "It ain't gonna get that far. If we don't get our hatch open in four minutes and our asses down to the surface, then we're going to be shredded like cheese up here. End of debate. Venus, let's open the door."

\* \* \*

THREE MINUTES LATER, the lead being watched in satisfaction as the hatch to the lander began to open.

As he did, another being gracefully hopped into place next to him holding several shovels. As the granular lunar soil settled back into place around his boots, he looked over at his commander in anticipation.

While never taking his eyes off the hatch, the commander shook his head and spoke in a very deep-voiced German.

"No, Heinz. We will not be needing the shovels this time. This is an *American* spacecraft. We have a long history with these dogs, and our Führer has plans for them. Once that use is exhausted, we will put them out of their mongrel misery."

\* \* \*

AS THE FIRST American TO STAND upon the lunar surface since 1972, Stewart's mind was a jumble of rushed, incoherent, and increasingly frightened thoughts.

While still holding onto the ladder of the lander with his left hand, Stewart was in awe to look down and see that both of his feet were standing upon the surface of the moon.

The *moon*.

A dream come true now murdered by the nightmare that was approaching him from both sides.

As his body was still reacting to the one-sixth gravity of Earth, one of the beings walked over to him, grabbed him by the shoulders, and violently turned him around.

Ian Stewart looked up and was certain he was staring into the eyes of his own executioner. At six feet, four inches tall, Stewart was looking into the face of a creature at least two feet taller than him and over one hundred pounds heavier.

Without saying a word and with a look of pure hate upon its face, the creature grabbed Stewart around the neck with its massive right hand and threw him through the air in the direction of the closest eight-wheeled vehicle.

As Stewart was silently bouncing across the lunar surface, the creature next reached up, grabbed the right leg of Venus Washington who had just exited the lander, and viciously pulled her down to the surface.

Instantly upon seeing that it was a woman, the creature opened his eyes wide in shocked disapproval and made a derogatory comment to his fellow beings.

As several of them laughed and answered him through their helmet speakers, he grabbed Washington by the shoulders and threw her toward six of the advancing beings.

While she was still in the air, he said, "See for yourselves. See the insult the American swine inflict upon us and our world! This woman will personally pay for their affront to us and the Fatherland."

# 16

Bella Esposito was the deputy director of communications at NASA.

Beyond that, she simply loved to solve puzzles and minutely examine photos and videos for any kind of mysterious object or clue others would miss.

Without ever telling anyone, back in the day she spent hours after work pouring over the photos and videos sent back from the unmanned rovers on Mars.

While she would never admit it to anyone—herself included at times—she was always secretly hoping to spot some tiny artifact in the Martian soil that would prove that an intelligent alien species once walked the Red Planet millions of years before humans on Earth.

Though the searches always proved futile, her excitement for the chase never waned.

Since the abrupt and complete loss of signal from the American lunar lander and carrier rocket three days earlier, she had been going over every inch of the video not only broadcast to the general public during the landing but, more importantly, the video *not* released to the public and the media in the hour or so prior to the loss of signal.

Within that classified video, Bella was afforded a 360-degree high-definition view of the lunar landscape for hundreds of yards to miles in each direction, thanks to the mini-cameras strategically placed around the bottom of the lander.

At seven the next morning, with steam wafting out from the black coffee in her white NASA mug, she pushed her long, prematurely gray hair away from her eyes and began to go over all the video footage within five minutes before the loss of signal.

With the help of her computer software, it had been magnified five times its original size.

As the video played, she leaned down in her darkened office to take a sip of coffee. As she did, out of the corner of her eye, she thought she detected the tiniest of movement in the upper left-hand corner of the fifty-inch monitor she had been staring at for hours on end.

She put her mug back down on the desk, rewound the video, and watched it again. Then again, and again, and again.

The fourth time with a large handheld magnifying glass.

"No fucking way," she whispered to herself as she rewound the video yet again.

In the dark shadow of a large rock outcropping one mile from the American lander was—at least it *looked* like—some kind of large multi-wheeled vehicle.

She isolated that corner of the video and typed in instructions for the computer to enhance the image as much as possible.

Bella then hit the print button.

As the image was being printed on 8x10 high-quality photo paper, a symbol at the center of the vehicle hidden in the shadows began to emerge.

Because the computer enhancement was using connect-the-dots technology to fill in some of the blanks, there was still a chance it was wrong. But, even at that, only a 2 percent chance.

Bella was now standing over the printer tray. When the photo plopped down, she took one look at the computer-enhanced image and screamed "holy fuck" as loud as she could before grabbing the photo.

Just as she was halfway finished sprinting down the hallway to the administrator of NASA's office, every network at once broke into regular programming to announce that—inconceivably—two nuclear explosions had just occurred.

One in a desolate part of China and the other 120 miles to the southeast of the Bahamas.

\* \* \*

WHILE BELLA ESPOSITO STOOD FROZEN in shock in the NASA hallway at the news now blaring from every television in the administrator's suite, two sleek black spacecraft were leaving lunar orbit at an ever-accelerating rate of speed on a direct trajectory path toward their target in a 270-mile orbit above the Earth.

That target being the International Space Station.

Though the Russians and the Americans still used the now three-decade-old station for the occasional mission and series of experiments, much of it had been dedicated as a playground for the super rich on Earth willing to pay tens of millions each to play "astronaut" in space.

They had been rotating in and out for the last few years on such a regular and lucrative basis that the collective sum paid for Operation Hedonism, as it was referred to in laughing confidence within the American and Russian space complexes, had already exceeded $500 million.

At the moment, the station housed a multibillionaire adventurer and his wife from Britain, as well as the two Russian cosmonauts assigned to transport and babysit them. The two tough military men were already beyond sick of the snobbish and entitled couple who constantly reminded them that "we could buy and sell Moscow if we felt like it."

Hollywood celebrities, business tycoons, or the Housewives of New York aside, the target for the Nazi astronauts was not the International Space Station or those now inhabiting it—who would all be dead in a matter of seconds once the hull of the station was breached—but rather the Soyuz spacecraft docked to it.

A spacecraft soon to become the host carrier to the worst of all disease. Nuclear annihilation.

# 17

Carolina Garcia took a deep breath and let it out very slowly. As president of the United States in an age of deepening divisions, imploding economies, and an increasingly troubled world, she had grown accustomed to a steady diet of bad to horrific news. It came with the job. That said, even with her now understandably resigned disposition, she was still not capable of digesting the news just relayed to her.

Ghastly and surreal did not come close to describing it.

Garcia sat at the head of a long mahogany conference table in the Roosevelt Room of the White House just across the hall from the Oval Office. As she sat in her chair, she drummed her pencil off the highly polished wood as she looked at the two women and two men sitting with her.

Sharon Bentley was a forty-eight-year-old African-American and the director of the Federal Bureau of Investigation. Years earlier, she had paid for her college tuition by winning the Miss District of Columbia contest and then finishing as second runner-up in the

Miss America contest. Though over two decades removed from her crown, she still retained the stunning looks that made her a regular in the bold-name section of the *Washington Post*.

Mike Jensen was considered many things. But good looking was not one of them. The fifty-eight-year-old secretary of defense was all of five feet, seven inches tall, about thirty pounds overweight, had a shaved head that he complimented with a full dyed-brown beard, favored black suits, crisp white dress shirts, and colorful suspenders and neck ties, and could honestly not care less what people thought of his looks.

The reason Jensen had been picked as secretary of defense had less to do with his actual qualifications and everything to do with his friendship with the president. Back when Garcia had been a member of Congress representing Houston, Jensen had come into her orbit.

Jensen had indeed been in the military. He retired as a "full-bird" colonel from the United States Army after twenty-four years of service in the military police. Upon retirement, he returned to his native Houston and became deputy chief of police.

It was in that capacity that he had first met Carolina Garcia. One of her young aides had been an innocent bystander killed in the crossfire between two rival gangs, and Jensen not only personally took over the case but never rested until the shooter was caught, tried, convicted, and imprisoned.

From that day forward, they stayed in touch. Two years after he became the chief of police, she was elected president of the United States.

Garcia trusted him implicitly, and no matter how much her defense and military experts objected, he was her only choice for secretary of defense.

Next was Timothy Shannon. An Air Force Academy graduate and the youngest administrator in the history of NASA. Like

Jensen, he had a Garcia connection. After four years in the Air Force flying fighter jets, he came back to Texas and ran for Congress in the district next to Garcia's.

Because they were both from the Lone Star State, both from the same political party, and both like-minded in their ideological and policy beliefs, they became a team of sorts and powerful advocates for the people of their districts.

Since he was still single, and she was recently divorced, the *Houston Chronicle*—among others—speculated that their "friendship" might be stronger than admitted.

During one of their many conversations on a flight from Washington, DC, back to Texas, Shannon told her he had been a "space geek" since he was a kid and always dreamed of becoming the administrator of NASA.

Two weeks after she was elected president, the thirty-eight-year-old Shannon was named to that position.

Last of the four in the Roosevelt Room was Michelle Sun. She was a real political trailblazer. While she was the second woman to be named director of the Central Intelligence Agency, she was the first Asian-American, and most proudly for her, the first openly gay director.

President Garcia was very progressive in her personal and political beliefs, and had never made any efforts to hide that fact.

Life had forced her to walk to the beat of her own drummer since childhood, and she knew she was a better person for it. Her life experiences made her far different from any other president before her.

A difference, she thought—as she looked around the Roosevelt Room of the White House—that was about a million miles away from her ultra-poor upbringing in a forgotten housing project in Houston where she'd lived with her single mother and baby brother.

# 18

Garcia's mother had come to Houston from Mexico City when she was but seventeen years old in search of a job and a better life.

While not a "legal" crossing, it was one her mother knew was a moral imperative.

Her mother's cousin worked as a waiter in the restaurant of a Marriott Hotel on the outskirts of the city, and managed to get her mother a job there as a dishwasher.

Two months into the job, she fell in love with a fast-talking and charming waiter by the name of Juan-Pablo Garcia. Three weeks after that, she became pregnant with Carolina. Three months after the birth of Carolina, she found she was pregnant yet again.

Two days after telling Juan-Pablo of the news of the second pregnancy, he walked out on her and baby Carolina and disappeared back into the millions of faces of Mexico City.

As she got older, young Carolina came to realize that the word "hero" had been watered down and cheapened over the years, as it was bestowed upon everyone for every little and insignificant accomplishment.

By the time she was thirteen years old and a freshman in a tough inner-city Houston public high school, Carolina came to realize a very special truth. A truth that told her that she was living with the personification of a true hero.

Her mother.

A single mom who, for as long as she could remember, worked two or three jobs at a time to try and provide for her and her baby brother, Gilberto.

A woman who somehow managed to work her way into becoming the catering manager of one of Houston's top golf and country clubs.

A club where young Carolina soon began to caddie for the incredibly wealthy members. One of whom was a former star outfielder for the Houston Astros. A man who began his baseball career in the Mexican leagues and never forgot where he came from or the generosity and kindness of the Mexican people.

In young Carolina, he not only saw real promise but a child who had an incredible gift for mathematics and numbers.

Once Carolina became a junior in high school, the former Astros outfielder told her that he was nominating her for the Evans Scholars Foundation, a world-renowned nonprofit in Illinois that provided full tuition and housing scholarships to poor and academically gifted golf caddies.

Carolina not only qualified for the prestigious scholarship but was accepted by Harvard soon thereafter.

Five years after that, she was back in Houston as part of an investment team for one of the bigger banks. Two years after that, she felt a calling to give back to the poor of Houston. On her first try, she was elected to the city council. Three years later, she was elected to the House of Representatives.

And four years after that, the country was crying out for a candidate who could not only heal the political, racial, and economic divides but bring true honor back to the White House.

With no ego whatsoever, Carolina truly felt it her duty to try. The rich were getting too rich, and the poor were getting pushed closer and closer to the abyss.

With her mother at her side, and speaking more Spanish than English at times, Garcia barnstormed the United States. In doing so, she made a deep and lasting connection with those Americans who had never been given a place at the table.

Poor, disenfranchised, and discriminated-against Americans in desperate need of a champion.

Americans who knew that Garcia was one of them.

As a divorced forty-one-year-old now single mother of two young children, Garcia may not have been the "perfect" candidate, but for a large majority of voters, she was the best candidate.

A candidate they overwhelming elected president of the United States.

And now...and now....

President Garcia shook her head to clear it of the flashing stroll down memory lane and focused on the here and now.

The *now* being just twenty-four hours after unclaimed nuclear bombs had been detonated in an obvious act of aggression, or worse...outright war.

She had already briefly addressed the nation once, and she knew that was but the beginning.

# 19

As President Garcia looked down again at the 8x10 photo Tim had brought with him from NASA, she knew there was simply no way what the four of them were telling her could be true. *Less* than no way.

It was a deep-fake joke. Someone's idea of the most obscene prank ever played.

Just thinking about it made her skin crawl.

A *swastika*, she thought. A *Nazi* swastika? On the moon?

"Give me a break," she said out loud without realizing it.

\* \* \*

No break would be forthcoming.

As they sat just feet from the Oval Office, evidence was still coming to them in real time every few minutes. Evidence that was confirming an unimaginable nightmare.

President Garcia insisted she meet with the four people she most trusted before adjourning to the Situation Room on the ground floor of the West Wing.

A top-secret room full of top-secret people who were confused, panicked, and top-secret scared shitless.

* * *

AS THE PRESIDENT PICKED UP the photo to stare at it again, her brown eyes, which were normally always expressive and bright, clouded over in fear and uncertainty.

"Timothy," said Garcia as she looked up from the most evil image she had ever seen. "Tell me again what you said to me from the car on your drive over here."

"Yes, Madam President," answered Shannon with a hint of deeply personal pain he was feeling for the woman opposite him. "As has now been confirmed, both our returning spacecraft and that of the Chinese had relatively small nuclear weapons placed inside of them…"

"About the equivalent of twenty kilotons of TNT," interrupted Michelle Sun. "Approximately the same force as the bombs dropped over Hiroshima and Nagasaki."

"Correct," answered Shannon as he continued. "As for the photo we are all looking at, and the 'impossible' reality it may convey, my two best rocket experts tell me it's not out of the realm of possibility that the Nazis could have somehow pulled off something like this. As they reminded me, if this is true and the Nazis did manage to somehow launch a manned rocket…"

"Or more than one," jumped in Sun again. "Based on the intelligence we are picking up from the Russians, who seem to be debating whether to bury a report they have with regard to what one of their forward observation teams observed just as they were closing in on Peenemünde in May of 1945."

"...that," continued Shannon without missing a beat, "in reality, it would have happened not too many years before the Nazi rocket scientists we grabbed from Peenemünde came up with their own rocket capable of reaching the moon. Even at that time, it was well known that Wernher von Braun was more of a managing engineer than a true rocket scientist. That the Nazis had some young, true genius rocket scientists at Peenemünde is a fact. Could one or more of them have come up with a rocket capable of carrying humans to the moon in 1945? Well..."

Shannon trailed off as he tapped on the photo before them all.

President Garcia ran her fingers through her thick auburn hair and shook her head once again as if to clear it.

"All right. For the purpose of this discussion, let's assume these monsters are in fact up there. With what? Some kind of little 'survivalist' base hidden under the surface? Or are they like those lone Japanese soldiers they were still finding hidden in caves in the South Pacific in the 1950s and '60s who still believed the war was going on and were prepared to die for the emperor?"

Shannon was about to answer when Secretary of Defense Jensen leaned forward with an answer.

"Carolina," he said to his longtime friend. "It has to be much more extensive than that. Much more. If true, and again a photo is worth a thousand words," stressed the SecDef as he pointed at the image resting in the middle of the table, "then reality says they have been up there for eighty-four years. Almost a *century* on the moon. Over eight decades to burrow in, build, perfect their science, and...breed. If one were to follow the logical pattern based on the scant evidence we have, they could have one or more 'moon cities' up there. Not bases. But *cities*. We need to remember that the moon used to be part of the Earth billions of years ago. When it separated from the Earth, it took most, if not all, of our precious minerals with it. Minerals our own mining companies have been begging to get to for the last few years. Minerals those Nazis, or whoever they are, have had access to for the last eight decades. However advanced their science or mining is, it is still clearly good enough to build the lunar rover in the photo and at least two nuclear weapons. Beyond that, there is now little or no doubt that they executed precision military operations to commandeer both our spacecraft as well as that of the Chinese."

As Garcia was trying to process that poison, Shannon added to the dose.

"Madam President. In many ways, the United States has become a prisoner to its advanced technology. As it stands now, there is no nation on Earth more dependent upon its satellites in low and geosynchronous orbit for its national and economic security than us. No nation. Ironically, we were always worried about China taking out our satellites and rendering us blind and defenseless. But now..."

"But now, *what?*" asked the clearly agitated president.

"But now," answered Jensen solemnly, "the new reality we may have to face instantly is that neither the United States nor the planet Earth...can be *defended* from the Earth."

Just as the president was about to respond to Jensen, the door to the Roosevelt Room was slammed open as retired four-star general Peter McNamara burst through before stopping two feet inside the room.

All five people sitting at the conference table—including the president—jumped a little or a lot, depending on how much they were startled by the violent entrance.

President Garcia instantly gathered herself and looked up in worry and fright at her national security advisor. A man who had personally survived four tours of heavy combat as a Special Forces soldier and commander, rose to the rank of four-star general, and was now standing before her with all of the color drained from his face and tears clearly forming in his eyes.

"Peter," said the president as she rose to walk toward him. "What is it? What happened?"

As the battle-hardened general started to wobble on his feet, Shannon jumped up and joined with the president in grabbing him by his shoulders and guiding him to a chair.

As they did, Jensen quickly poured a glass of water and handed it to the silver-haired general, who drank it in one swallow before closing his eyes in an attempt to compose himself.

Five seconds later—which seemed like five hours to the others in the room—the national security advisor turned to the president, who was now retaking her own chair, and answered her question.

"Madam President. There has been another nuclear explosion."

"Where?" asked Jensen, cutting off the president, who was about to ask the same question.

The general turned to look at Jensen before twisting back to refocus his attention on the president.

"Vladivostok, Russia."

"Holy shit," cried out CIA Director Sun. "A major city. The first two were relatively harmless. But now…they've dialed it up and hit a fuckin' city."

One of the many strengths of President Garcia was her incredible capacity to get more calm and clear-headed as life situations became more crazed, chaotic, and seemingly unsolvable.

It was a rare talent she discovered as a desperately poor child who had to continually compartmentalize one hope-crushing pain after the other in order to function and help her mom.

A talent she had only improved upon over the years into adulthood.

"Language, Michelle," admonished the president with just the hint of a forgiving smile.

She then turned her full attention back on her national security advisor, who seemed back to his normal self.

"What do we know, Peter?"

The general reached over and grabbed the ice-filled crystal pitcher of water and poured himself half a glass more, which he also finished in one swallow before answering the president in his now customarily confident and deep voice.

"First, my apologies for my emotions, Madam President. The initial reports we are getting out of Moscow are over one hundred thousand killed in the blast, with tens of thousands more expected to die from the radiation."

President Garcia reached over and put her hand atop his. "Oh my God. Over one hundred thousand men, women, and children… murdered."

"Yes," the national security advisor said. "As with the first two attacks, it appears they used one of our own spacecraft as the vehicle to deliver their bomb. Now, it was a Soyuz spacecraft docked to the International Space Station. This time, though, there was a difference. They—whoever *they* really may be—reprogrammed the automatic landing coordinates of the Soyuz to bring it down directly into the city."

"The ISS," half whispered NASA Administrator Shannon. "But that would mean that they traveled from the surface of the moon to just above the Earth's atmosphere. Which also means…"

"…that every single one of our satellites really *is* at risk," said the president as she finished the sentence for Shannon. "And with them, our national and financial security, and…way of life."

"Precisely, Madam President," answered McNamara.

President Garcia slowly stood and then looked, one by one, at the five other people in the room. As she did, her eyes narrowed down to slits as a fire of controlled anger seemed to burst into life within them.

"General," she said to McNamara as he and the others stood with her. "I need to speak with the presidents of Russia and China as soon as you can make the call happen. After that, I will need to speak with the prime minister of Israel. We must share all we have with her, Mossad, and their space program. It appears war has been declared upon the planet Earth, and at this moment— whether anyone likes it or not—we are all going to have to either be on the same team or...perish one by one because of stupid, nationalistic pride."

# 20

As she stood waiting for the calls to be arranged between herself and the leaders of Russia, China, and Israel, President Garcia stood and looked over at the NASA Administrator.

"Timothy," said the president in a soft voice. "If you would be so kind as to join me in my study, I'd like to speak with you for a moment."

As Shannon stood, Michelle Sun and Sharon Bentley looked at each other with suspicious, knowing, and somewhat disapproving reactions.

Mike Jensen saw the exchange, instantly cleared his throat, and looked from one woman to the other.

"The fate of the world may soon hang in the balance. It's critical that we all stay as focused as possible on the crisis before us."

Without acknowledging anyone or even looking over at the director of the FBI or the head of the CIA, the president simply afforded herself a slight and grateful smile at the admonishment provided by Jensen before gathering her notebook and water and walking out of the room.

Shannon followed the president out of the Roosevelt Room, took a right, and walked twenty feet and through the now open door into the president's private study.

Although Hollywood and much of the general public always placed any president behind the desk in the Oval Office, the truth was that most presidents only used the Oval Office for ceremonial duties.

All preferred the study off to the side of the Oval Office. It was private, discreet, and out of bounds to everyone. Even, and especially, staff.

As Shannon stepped past the two imposing Presidential Protection Division agents of the United States Secret Service standing watch outside the door, the one closer to him quietly and quickly whispered, "Thank you. She needs you now."

Human beings were human beings. No matter the title, the privilege, the fame, or the money, all people shared basic human emotions. Some more readily than others.

As has been documented in the media throughout the history of the White House, some presidents got along really well with the Secret Service and formed a tight—and often emotional—bond with their agents.

And some famously did not, and looked upon the Secret Service agents as nothing more than expendable staff to step in front of a bullet if and when needed.

Carolina Garcia was beloved by her Secret Service detail. As a single mother, she constantly went out of her way to remember their birthdays, their anniversaries, and the names of their children.

She invited them and their families to functions in the presidential residence and treated them as the family she believed them to be.

Garcia had never forgotten where she came from or how cruel and fickle life truly could be. The men and women of the United States Secret Service were literally putting their lives on the line to protect hers and her children, and she was continually amazed by their professionalism, dedication, and character.

The Secret Service used a call sign for every president, and for Carolina Garcia they had chosen "Yellow Rose." It was in recognition of her favorite flower, as well as the enduring theme song of her home state of Texas.

While the *Washington Post*, the *Hill*, Politico, Fox News, CNN, and others openly speculated on the relationship between the president and the young administrator of NASA, the Secret Service knew the truth.

That truth being that they were a relatively young couple desperately trying to keep their private lives private.

To a person, the Presidential Protection Division of the Secret Service was beyond protective of "Yellow Rose," and had realized over the course of the last few months that Shannon was not only good for her, but truly made the president happy.

After Shannon stepped into the private study, the agent softly closed the door behind him and then whispered into the microphone at the end of his suit sleeve.

When Shannon turned from the door, he found Garcia literally shaking uncontrollably.

He covered the five steps between them in one second, and folded the woman he now loved into his arms.

Shannon believed Garcia to be the mentally strongest and most capable person he had ever known. Ever. That said, the daunting and sometimes horrifying duties of the president of the United States were unimaginable to most people.

Heavy is the head that wears the crown.

She was now wearing the heaviest crown in the history of humankind.

Within a matter of but a few hours, Garcia was confronted with the news of three hostile nuclear weapons being detonated, over one hundred thousand human beings killed, and the very real possibility that the Earth was now totally defenseless and could soon be attacked by monsters from the most surreal nightmare ever spawned by history.

Without a word being said, Shannon stroked Garcia's auburn hair and held her to his chest until the shaking began to slow down and then stop.

The president gently pushed back from his embrace and looked him in the eye.

"Thank you, Tim. I love you *so* much."

"I love you more, sweetheart. I truly do."

She took in a deep breath, held it for a moment, and then ever so slowly exhaled before reaching out her hands to hold Shannon's.

"Okay. Let's go figure out a way to obliterate these Nazi mutants."

# 21

Venus Washington felt the palpitations of her heart as sweat poured down her spine released by the pure terror she was now experiencing.

As she desperately fought to get her hyperventilating breath under control, she looked down at the floor of the alien vehicle they were now riding in and quickly closed her eyes at the sight of Robert Marshall laying most certainly lifeless upon it.

With one swing of an impossibly mammoth fist, one of the creatures had not only broken Marshall's space helmet to pieces but definitely killed him in the process.

Before shutting her eyes, Washington unfortunately took in the pool of blood congealing around Marshall's mangled, motionless face.

With her eyes still closed—and wet with tears—Washington heard one of the creatures shift his feet on the coarse metal floor of the eight-wheeled vehicle as she flinched in fear.

As soon as she did, she was treated to a chorus of guttural, evil laughter from the seven creatures left in the cabin. Included in that number were—as far as she could tell—two females.

As she pressed her knees tightly together in a defensive position, she felt the guilt wash over her in accompaniment to the sweat.

No sooner had the gargantuan creatures dragged and thrown her, Marshall, and Stewart into the vehicle before closing the door to the hostile lunar environment than one of the males reached his right hand down to his groin and began to rub it while his left hand reached out to squeeze Washington's breasts under her space suit.

Both Robert Marshall and Ian Stewart reacted in instant, directed rage to the assault on their colleague. But the immediate consequences of their actions were a literal lifetime apart.

Two of the creatures were behind Stewart, and they simply grabbed him by the shoulders and slammed him against a window as he tried to leap forward.

Because Marshall had been slightly in front of Washington when the creature touched her breasts, he was close enough to swing down with his arm against that of the creature.

While everything happened in a flash at that point, to Washington, it was as if Marshall had passively hit a massive concrete support beam with a paper straw.

The creature yelled in fury at Marshall's swat while simultaneously propelling his fist into Marshall's helmet and head. Washington had no doubt that Marshall was dead before his body bounced several times off the floor before settling into its current state.

What happened next only intensified the terror she was feeling within the freakish nightmare that had taken them prisoner.

Seeing what had happened, the commander of the creatures— who had just settled himself into the right front seat next to the driver—screamed out in German at the one who assaulted her and killed Marshall.

Just as quickly, he yelled something to the driver, then stood from his seat to walk back toward them.

In a blur of controlled violence, he seemed to depressurize the cabin; then he opened the exit door of the vehicle, shoved the creature who killed Marshall and touched her breasts out the door, pulled a handheld weapon from a holster attached to his right leg, shot the creature who was tumbling across the lunar soil with some kind of reddish projectile that all but vaporized the target into an instant ball of flaming body gases and parts, slammed the door closed, and resumed his seat up front.

As the mind-numbing, still not-possible-to-be-true scenario played out, with her and Ian Stewart being transported in a Nazi vehicle to some unknown destination, it was now obvious to Washington in the most graphic of ways that they were not to be seriously harmed—until…someone gave the order to do exactly that.

# 22

As the spider-looking vehicle sped toward its destination, Ian Stewart tried to look around the two enormous beings who had him pinned in a back corner seat.

He was trying to make eye contact with Venus but could not see her. He shifted his body to try and get a better look and was rewarded for that action by having his still helmeted head bounced off one of the metal support beams by the humanoid closest to him.

With that, he was met with but the latest shock in this macabre ordeal.

From the front of the vehicle came the muffled word "STOP." Shouted out in...*English*.

The two beings holding him down looked toward the front of the vehicle and saw their commander stand.

He had taken off his helmet and gloves, and the very first image that popped into the mind of Stewart was that he was staring at an eight-foot-plus-tall version of the Ivan Drago character from the *Rocky IV* movie.

"Holy shit" were the first two words to form in Stewart's scrambled mind.

As the commander walked toward the back, he motioned at his two colleagues holding Stewart.

They released their viselike grip on him but kept him boxed between them.

The commander then stopped in front of Washington, bent down and unclasped her helmet, and took it off.

"I am sorry for what my soldier did in killing your comrade," said the commander as he looked down at the petrified face of Washington. "Also, while we see you as less than the human you are, we still have our orders. He violated those orders and as you saw…was punished."

As the commander turned to face him, Stewart unclasped and took off his own helmet. He would be damned if he was going to let that *thing* do it.

He then tried to stand but was slammed back down into the seat by the "soldiers" on both sides of him.

"I imagine," said the hulking super-Aryan-race commander with a twisted smile of superiority as he shifted his gaze from Washington to Stewart, "that first, you are shocked that I speak English. And second, that you may still believe yourselves to be in some dreamlike state and that when you wake up, all will be normal. I assure you, first, that you are already wide awake, and second that what you see before you *is* normal. At least…the new and forever lasting normal—"

Before he could continue, Stewart cut him off.

"You are anything but norm—"

As the first syllables tumbled out of Stewart's mouth, the commander motioned with his finger at the soldiers guarding the American. At the gesture, one instantly grabbed Stewart by the back of his head and slammed his face and mouth quickly into the support beam, splitting his lower lip while sending a stream of bright red blood splattering across the interior wall of the vehicle.

"Oh," laughed the commander as Stewart slumped in his seat. "My apologies for not telling you. You are not allowed to address me unless I ask you to do so. *Ever.* Now…where was I…"

Stewart forced himself to sit up straight as he held the back of his gloved hand against his lip to try and stem the flow of blood. As he did, he felt light-headed from the blow by the Nazi soldier.

He knew the commander was speaking again but was not quite sure of the words. But then, he knew he didn't have to be sure. He fully understood the message just delivered to him and remained silent as his mind began to clear.

"What are you Americans fond of saying?" asked the Nazi commander in his booming voice. "That life is nothing if not ironic. Well, how very true in this case. When you Americans first landed here on the moon in 1969, our lunar leader at the time believed that the landing might signal the end of us as a people. *The end.* We had been on the moon for almost a quarter of a century at that point after escaping the Russian vermin about to overrun our Fatherland. A quarter of a century. During that time, the first generation of Nazi Lunarians was born. And then another. But when you Americans landed in 1969, our leader thought it was the beginning of the end for us. That you would send rocket after rocket with your astronauts, discover us, and then hunt us down like animals…"

Stewart could finally see Venus through the tree-trunk legs of the Nazi commander. He was trying to make eye contact with her, but her head was bowed down with her eyes cast to the floor.

"…so, now sixty years ago, my lunar ancestors did the best they could to prepare for your invasion. *But*…it was an invasion which *never* came. Never. Imagine our shock. Five more times over the next three years, you Americans landed your pathetic little spacecraft. Each time, with only two astronauts. Silly little weaklings walking around—then driving around—collecting silly little rocks. Rocks…" laughed the Nazi commander.

At the sound of the Nazi's condescending laughter, Venus lifted her head for a moment. When she did, Stewart immediately shot her a quick wink and the hint of a smile.

She ever so slightly nodded her head in return before dropping it again to stare at the floor.

"…all the riches buried within the moon and you Americans were collecting rocks and hitting golf balls. Then, come 1972 you left and…never came back. *Never.* No invasion. No threats to our existence. No worries. *Ironically*…see how I came back to that word…ironically, you ended up helping us more than you can ever imagine. We have been here since 1945 and with every probe and every spacecraft you landed, our scientists—and remember, we had the very best in the world—went out and took them apart piece by piece. We not only replicated your technology but exceeded it in factors you will soon see for yourself. Beyond your technology, you gave us the greatest gift of all—*time.* You gave us the decades we needed to grow strong, the decades needed to breed, the decades needed to advance our science well beyond anything on Earth, the decades needed to build our space fleet, the decades needed to perfect our nuclear weapons, to…"

The Nazi commander suddenly looked down at Venus and screamed.

"Look at me when I talk, you worthless American scum!"

Stewart went to jump up but was dragged back down into the corner.

As he saw Venus snap her up head to look at the Nazi in renewed terror, Stewart realized that he had been lulled into a false sense of security by the Nazi commander's tone and almost flawless English. In that instant, he not only realized how truly foolish he was but that the abomination of a man before him was nothing more than a psychopath biding his time until he could exterminate that scum at his feet.

"Now...where was I," continued the Nazi with his twisted smirk and calming voice back in place. "Oh, yes. Outlining how you—shall we now call you *Earthlings*—have sealed your own fate. More than giving us the decades needed to grow strong here on the moon and develop our science and weapons, you gave us the time needed to identify your only weakness that mattered to us. And we found it. That being your complete and utter dependence on your satellites for survival on Earth. You gave us the time to identify each and every one you Americans, the Russians, and now the Chinese depend on for your military and economic survival. Every one. Soon, we will destroy each of them and you will be worse off than a blind man stumbling through the darkest of caves. Our Führer has rightfully determined that this time, you *do* represent a threat to our survival. And it is for that reason you and your kind must be exterminated."

With that, the Nazi commander turned to walk back to his seat at the front of the moving vehicle, which had just entered the foothills of a mountain range.

Suddenly, he whirled back around and bent forward until his greatly outsized face was but inches from that of Venus Washington's.

He then placed his gargantuan hands upon her shoulders.

"Oh," he said as he looked into her now bulging eyes. "I neglected to tell you that the extermination process has already begun, as we just killed over one hundred thousand of your fellow Earthlings with the first of our nuclear weapon attacks. Tens of thousands down. A few billion to go."

At that, he let go of her and made an exaggerated fuss of wiping his "soiled" hands off on the front of his space suit.

As the commander settled back into his seat, Venus Washington screamed in shock at an evil her mind could not grasp. As she curled up into a fetal position on the floor, the vehicle entered a deep shadow of the first of a number of towering mountains.

# 23

Panic. Fear. Wild rumors. And terrible decisions.

Social media was exceptionally good at creating and spreading all four and was now saturating the globe with its rhetorical poison.

Three nuclear weapons detonated became "ten." Tens of thousands killed and suffering in Russia became "millions."

There were so many hundreds of YouTube videos being uploaded by the minute from Russia that the entire system crashed.

Or...maybe not. Maybe, according to the online conspiracy theorists, "one of our evil governments" took it down for "their own nefarious reasons."

Such was but one of the hundreds of rumors given birth by the nuclear attacks that were being latched onto—and instantly spread—by millions of scared, confused, and ill-informed people.

In the United States, all regular programming on every network, cable network, and local news affiliate had been cancelled. It was replaced by nonstop conjecture, wild guesses, and outright accusations being offered up by the talking heads populating those media outlets.

Breathless commentators now blurted out that "China just nuked Russia," "Russia just nuked China," "the United States just nuked Russia and China," and "all-out nuclear war is inevitable."

Two minutes after that last bit of journalistic speculation, the stock market crashed and all trading was suspended.

Within a matter of hours, every grocery chain in the United States had run out of supplies as their shelves were emptied. Beyond that, "outdoor" stores were cleaned out of tents, sleeping bags, backpacks, freeze-dried food, home generators, and especially...guns and ammunition.

Every gas station was drained of its last drop of fuel.

And every bank in the country was ordered closed to prevent the predictable run on deposits that had already begun.

The "high ground" of the hills and mountains was suddenly a premium...and would eventually be fought for and...defended.

Survivalists began to scream and preen: "We told you so."

First a trickle, then tens of thousands of citizens began to self-evacuate themselves from one part of the country to the other. Most left from the major cities the internet told them were the "next most obvious targets" to the closest rural areas or mountainous terrain.

At least they tried, until traffic came to a complete standstill across every major and minor highway of the United States.

Just a few hours since the last nuclear attack in Russia, and most of the world was frozen solid in panic.

\* \* \*

AT LEAST FOR THE MOMENT, Colonel William Richards didn't have to worry about traffic.

Seven hours earlier, he had been sound asleep in his bed at Vandenberg Air Force Base when his wife of twenty-one years gently shook him awake.

As he tried to force himself to concentrate after yet another eighteen-hour day of trying to have the relatively new United States Space Corps—formerly the abandoned Space Force in its first iteration—ready to meet its mandate from the White House and Congress, the six-foot, one-inch Richards ran his fingers through his thick but short black hair, then moved his hand down a few inches to wipe his bleary eyes and focus them on the glowing face of the phone Nancy was waving before him.

"It's the White House," she said in a whisper, even though she had the phone on mute. "I think she said she was the chief of staff."

* * *

WHAT A DIFFERENCE SEVEN HOURS CAN MAKE, thought Richards as he stepped off the gleaming white Air Force Gulfstream V that had just landed at Joint Base Andrews outside of Washington, DC, and was instantly escorted to a helicopter with rotors already whirring in anticipation of whisking him to the south lawn of the White House.

The president herself had demanded his immediate presence, and he felt it had much more to do with a paper he had written years ago than because of his current position as the vice commander of the United States Space Corps.

# 24

Ever since he was an eight-year-old boy in the small town of Superior, Arizona, Richards had always dreamed of becoming an astronaut and going into space.

Two things about him separated him from other children who settled on a "career path" at an early age. Unlike well over 90 percent of those children, Richards kept the same career dream. Never once wavering from it or changing his mind multiple times as was normal for most children and young people.

More than that, at eight years of age he had selected a goal to go along with his chosen career field. He wanted to walk, and live, on the moon.

Most of the young people who were interested in a career in the space business—which still represented a miniscule number—had bought into the nonstop glamorization of going to Mars.

From Hollywood to cable and web series to the media, it was always "Mars, Mars, Mars."

Not just as that young boy, but through four years of Air Force ROTC at Arizona State University, commissioned in the Air Force, and as he began flight school, Richards was always convinced that going to Mars was the most ignorant, foolish, wasteful, and short-sighted policy decision in the history of the US space program.

For Richards, the very idea of wasting upwards of $100 billion to mount a two-year round-trip mission to Mars to essentially plant a flag on the surface while staying two to four weeks at the most was governmental malpractice, and detrimental to the national and economic security of the people of the United States.

Richards had never bought into the hype and the hope that human beings would leave their flawed judgment, greed, and most especially military ambitions behind on Earth when they ventured out into space.

The edge of space was not some utopian magic curtain that transformed all who passed through into altruistic, peace-loving allies.

It was but the latest border leading to a hostile environment potentially filled with power, treasure, and answers beyond imagination.

Because space was such a costly, hostile, and critically important frontier, self-interests and various military objectives would eventually vault to the front of the line if for no other reason than, first, to protect the massive investments being made, second, to realize a return on those investments, and last, to claim the true ultimate "high ground."

To Richards, that ultimate high ground was from low Earth orbit to the surface of the moon and everything in between. It was Richards' steadfast belief that whoever controlled that territory could control the fate of the billions of people on the planet Earth.

He so much believed that to be true—in conjunction with believing that going to Mars was adversarial to the best interests of the United States—that he made combating an enemy based on the moon the subject of his thesis paper for his master of national security and strategic studies at the Naval War College in Newport, Rhode Island.

But buried in the thesis was a section that speculated on a "crazy urban myth" that had first been relayed to him by a professor and subsequently shared within the space community over the last few decades.

Richards was careful to address the myth as ridiculous, and only used it as a jumping-off point to ask hypothetical questions of a military nature, but deep down, he was troubled by some of the information he himself later uncovered.

But for the sake of his family and his career, in his paper he was careful to dismiss the myth out of hand as he outlined a fictional military strategy.

* * *

By the time the Air Force driver had picked him up at his home at Vandenberg, Richards was well aware that the shit had hit the fan in the worst of all possible ways.

All of the Earth was involved, and every human being was at immediate risk.

As the helicopter carrying him motored past the Washington Monument, the south lawn of the White House came rushing into view.

Weather-wise, it was a spectacular day in DC. Not a cloud in the sky as the White House gleamed whiter than white and the south lawn looked greener and lusher than any major league ballpark.

As the helicopter began to make a perfect three-point landing on the ten-foot-wide red circular disks placed upon the green lawn for exactly that purpose, Richards' mind flashed to the fact that he had never been to the White House. Not during a family trip, a school trip, or during his Air Force career.

As he stepped off the helicopter and looked toward the South Portico entrance to the White House, he paused and instantly wished he could be anywhere else.

Then, he thought of his wife, his two daughters in college, and the hundreds of thousands of human beings who had just been incinerated in Russia.

He then straightened his shoulders, pulled his dress jacket into place, took a deep breath, and walked with a purpose to what would turn out to be...his destiny.

# 25

National Security Advisor Peter McNamara greeted Richards at the entrance to the White House.

"Thanks for coming, Bill," said the former four-star general. "We are literally in a world of hurt."

"Yes, sir," replied Richards. "My honor. If I may ask, who exactly invited me?"

"I did," said McNamara as he put his hand on Richards' left arm and directed him toward the West Wing of the White House. "Actually, I mentioned you and your background to the president, and she told me to get your ass here ASAP. I remembered that paper you wrote while you were at the Naval War College. I've actually had it in a drawer in my home office ever since. As soon as I heard about the nukes in our returning spacecraft, I grabbed it, reread it, and well...here you are."

As McNamara double-timed him down through a set of double doors, Richards realized he was now walking on the West Colonnade past the actual Rose Garden that sat just outside the Oval

Office. Before he could locate the windows to the most famous office in the country, or even take in the world-famous garden for a second, they went through another set of double doors, came to a Secret Service checkpoint, took a left, walked past the cabinet room, then an immediate right across the West Wing lobby, and down a staircase to the ground floor level.

Once there, and after three more quick corners, the national security advisor escorted Richards into the Situation Room located just across the way from the White House Mess…which was the name for the most exclusive restaurant in the world.

Once Richards stepped into the Situation Room, he knew he was *way* out of his league.

Standing on either side of the conference table was the president of the United States, the vice president, the secretary of defense, the director of the FBI, the director of Homeland Security, the administrator of NASA, the head of the CIA, the director of the Defense Intelligence Agency, the chairman of the Joint Chiefs of Staff, plus the national security advisor to the president who had just escorted him into the room.

Once Richards walked farther into the room, the conversations instantly stopped and all eyes turned to him. As his mouth began to go dry from the exponentially rising nervousness he was feeling, one person alleviated his stress almost immediately.

That person being the president of the United States.

Carolina Garcia broke into a warm and genuine smile as she walked up to Richards and extended her right hand.

"Colonel Richards. How very nice of you to show up on such short notice. Now, before we say hello to the others, please allow me to walk you over to the goody table."

With that, she took him by the arm and walked him to the back of the room where a table awaited with two silver pots full of coffee, a wide variety of sodas, fruit juices, water, cookies, fruit, and boxes of M&M's with the seal of the president on them.

As Richards looked at the table not sure of the protocol, the president turned to face him as her smile grew warmer.

"Will you join me in a cup of coffee, Colonel?"

Richards' eyes instantly flicked to one of the silver coffeepots and then to the fine china cups and saucers next to it embossed with the seal of the president.

"Yes, Madam President. A black coffee sounds about perfect at the moment."

To Richards' utter amazement, the president of the United States was now pouring him a cup of coffee. *The president.* As he took in the sight, he realized that she was a strikingly beautiful woman. Basically, a Salma Hayek look-alike in face and figure with slightly lighter hair color.

He was not much for television—or politics—and had only seen her for fleeting moments during her presidency.

He now knew television did her no justice.

As he was coming to that conclusion, he heard someone speak his name.

It was the president.

Richards slightly but quickly shook his head to clear it of the fog and the increasing overload threatening to completely numb his mind.

"Yes, Madam President. I'm sorry."

She looked up at the former fighter pilot and NASA astronaut and smiled anew.

"Your coffee, Colonel."

As he took the cup and saucer from the president, she stepped a bit closer to him and lowered her voice.

"Colonel. I'm told you read the briefing background on the plane out here. This is about to be your room. *Your* room. I need you now.

Our *country* needs you. I need you to speak your mind. I need you to say exactly what you believe to be the complete and unvarnished truth. This is *your* world…or *worlds* to be more precise. I'm told you're not afraid to step on toes if you have to. Well, if that's the case, then my toes are nothing special, Colonel. Step on them if you have to. Don't be intimidated by the people in this room. Focus on me if need be. I need your real-life assessment based upon your real-life experience and your instincts. General McNamara believes you saw much of this coming years ago. So, suck down a good bit of that caffeine, Colonel, then buckle up your chinstrap. It's time to get your head in the game."

Richards did as he was told.

He took a long sip of the best black coffee he had ever tasted in his life, looked down at the kind but determined face of the president, and felt his mind and body snap back to the here and now.

"Yes, Madam President. Thank you. I'm ready when you are."

# 26

In spite of her fear and sense of impending doom, Venus Washington couldn't help but be fascinated as she watched the lunar landscape go past.

The *lunar landscape*.

With her head still bowed down, she had been able to shift her eyes just enough to have an unimpeded view out of the corner of the window closest to her.

The highly skilled geologist within her was clamoring to get out there to explore. The terrorized voice that had taken over most of her mind was telling her that she would soon be buried under that lunar landscape.

She chose to repress the fear and focus on the geology and… her job.

The vehicle they were traveling in was clearly now deep within the shadows of a lunar mountain range.

As she tried to peer into the shadows at the various rock formations, she heard the beings up front begin to speak German again.

But this time, their voices were calm. Practiced. They seemed to be going over a checklist. Next, she heard a voice through one of the speakers up front.

At that, the vehicle made a slow turn to the left and proceeded deeper and deeper into the shadows. After about what seemed like five hundred yards, it came to a complete stop.

Suddenly, out of the corner of her left eye, Washington detected a horizontal sliver of white light that appeared out of nowhere. Forcing and willing her head to move, she turned it ever so slightly to afford herself a better view through the front windows of the vehicle.

As she did, she braced her entire body for the physical blow to her head that would surely come once one of the creatures realized she had dared to move.

But none came.

She then understood that all were either involved in the process taking place before her or too busy watching it to notice the tiny movement of her head.

Before her, the horizontal sliver of light—now some thirty feet across—continued to grow...*vertically.* As it did, Venus saw it for what it was. An outer airlock door of some kind.

When the door was fully raised, the vehicle advanced forward some one hundred feet until it again came to a complete stop.

Once inside, she could feel the vibrations through the vehicle as the heavy and thick door, now behind them, began to close.

Seconds after the final thud of closure, she heard a hissing sound from within the chamber.

Oxygen, her mind told her. They were now pumping oxygen back into the chamber.

Once the hissing stopped, another airlock door opened before them. They drove forward and waited yet again. As the door behind them slammed down, they entered what would turn out to be the final airlock.

Three separate airlocks one after the other. These creatures certainly believed in safety and redundancy, she thought.

As that final door before them lifted up, Venus was able to think no more. At least not in a coherent, logical way.

Her mind was now that of a small child walking downstairs to realize that every gift imaginable and wanted was now laying beneath the Christmas tree waiting to be opened.

For the briefest of moments, awe took the place of fear and reason.

The vehicle had now come to rest on a clearly paved roadway. A roadway that extended before her as far as the eye could see. It was centered in the middle of what seemed to be an enormous tunnel. One as well lit and well built as anything she had ever driven through on Earth. Better, in fact.

Suddenly, a smile erupted on her face. A smile that she instantly wiped off lest it be seen by her captors and enrage them.

Internally, the smile grew wider and wider. The geologist within her realized *exactly* where they were. Exactly.

That being in a converted lava tube within and under the surface of the moon.

Over a decade before, NASA geologists and other scientists had become certain that lava tubes not only existed under the surface of the moon but might prove to be the ultimate gift for humans hoping to establish colonies there.

NASA scientists, geologists, and astronomers first became aware of that possibility when they spotted newly formed pits within the surface. Pits that had not been there before and clearly were not craters from a meteor impact.

After weeks and months of analysis, they became convinced that these pits were openings to a lava tube under the surface. The openings appearing much like a sinkhole on Earth.

These scientists quickly dubbed the openings "skylights," a name that had been used ever since.

Venus knew that the existence of lava tubes was the absolute game changer for those hoping to colonize the moon.

*The* game changer.

On Earth, lava tubes were generally measured in feet. The largest tens of feet across and tens of feet high. Beneath the surface of the moon, lava tubes were measured in yards and even miles.

Some were estimated to be a half a mile or more wide and several hundred yards high. Many leading into chambers several miles across and over a mile high.

Each lava tube could run tens of miles in length and connect to a series of other lava tubes. A prefabricated interconnected highway *under* the surface of the moon.

A human habitat *upon* the surface of the moon would have to deal with one of the harshest environments known to the solar system. Each two-week "day" would see temperatures hovering around 250 degrees Fahrenheit. Each two-week "night" offering up temperatures of 250 degrees below zero.

Aside from the deadly 500-degree swing in temperature, the lunar surface was constantly bombarded by a combination of lethal radiation and micrometeorites.

Not so beneath the surface within a lava tube.

In theory, Washington knew, bases and even colonies could be built beneath the surface in these lava tubes—massive chambers totally protected by hundreds of feet of lunar soil and rock from the never-ending environmental threats upon the surface.

*In theory*, Washington began to extrapolate before stopping in shock at the sight before her.

She forced her mind—and her fraying emotions—to realize that "theory" was now obviously...*fact*. The most traumatizing fact of her life.

A point driven home by the horror now unfurled before her.

That being the first of what turned out to be an endless series of Nazi swastika flags that came into view. Each one about fifty by thirty feet.

But it was not the sight of the flags that turned her blood ice cold, but rather the walkways sixty or so feet up on either side of the impossibly large tunnel.

There, on both sides, hundreds of these massive beings were gathered, dressed in the black uniforms formerly worn by the Gestapo of Nazi Germany.

Hundreds.

More frightening than that, Venus could see hundreds and hundreds more streaming down the walkways to get as close as possible to their vehicle.

It was then that she realized that she and Ian were, at best, new zoo animals to be poked and prodded with sticks.

And at worst, rabid animals to be put out of their misery.

# 27

President Garcia took a long, hard look up into the eyes of William Richards and nodded her head once. Satisfied at what she detected.

She then turned from the coffee and snack station to observe those in the room. As she did, the whispered conversations once again came to a halt.

"Shall we take our seats and get started," said the president as she walked toward her seat at the head of the table with her coffee in hand.

As she did, Richards made a beeline toward one of the seats lining the walls on both sides of the conference table. Seats provided for the "backbenchers," the staffers who were required to be there for their expertise but were not deemed important enough to be seated at the main table.

Richards was not only comfortable being a backbencher, he preferred it. He often felt the air was much cleaner just a few feet removed from a table full of political or corporate egos.

As he was about to sit, the president addressed him.

"Colonel Richards," she said with a smile. "Your seat is actually over here. Next to me."

Richards cleared his throat, altered his course, and took the chair the president herself just pulled out for him. The one to her immediate right as she sat at the head of the table.

As the others took their seats, the president leaned over toward Richards and whispered, "You've got this."

"Ladies and gentlemen," said the president. "The one luxury we don't have is time. No matter how surreal or 'impossible' it may be, the fact of the matter is that a remnant of the dying Nazi regime somehow got itself to the moon some eighty-four years ago around May of 1945. Some people, like Tim Shannon…" stressed the president as she nodded her head toward the administrator of NASA, "believe it's relatively easy to explain based upon the advanced rocket work being done at Peenemünde at that time and the insane safety risks the Nazis were willing to undertake. Others simply refuse to believe it's possible. Except…here we are, three nuclear explosions later."

Richards looked quickly around the table as the president spoke. There were no nonbelievers left. At least, not in that room. All eyes were on her, with several of those looking borderline scared out of their minds.

Richards had seen the look before. A look that translated into, "I will cut and run the first chance I get no matter my title or responsibilities to my nation." Richards actually smirked a bit with that last thought, knowing there was potentially no place safe on the planet Earth to run and hide.

For him, there were only two options: Either fight and potentially die. Or simply die like whimpering cowards.

"With time of the essence," continued the president, "I would like to introduce Colonel William Richards. As all of you know, the colonel was a highly decorated fighter pilot and then an astronaut before assuming his current duties as the vice commander of the United States Space Corps. But…it is not his impressive background which brings the colonel to us today. Rather, it is an obscure paper he wrote while at the Naval War College. A paper, coincidently enough, which outlined how both the United States, as well as the rest of the Earth, could and should defend itself if attacked from an enemy force on the moon. Amazingly, I'm told the colonel even used the Nazis as an example of a possible adversary. Colonel, the floor is yours."

\* \* \*

RICHARDS TURNED HIS HEAD to the left, nodded to the president, then turned to face those around the table. As he did, he took another sip of his now cooling coffee.

*The president was right*, he thought. *I've just got to be true to myself and say exactly what had been bottled up in me for years. Fuck it. What's the worst they could do? Fire me?* That would be a blessing at this point. He could go home to California and start digging a hole for him and his family to crawl into and wait to make their last stand.

"Thank you, Madam President. And thank all of you for your time and attention."

Richards turned his head to look back at Carolina Garcia.

"Madam President. With your permission, I'm going to get a bit informal and forget I'm the lowest ranking person in this room."

"Permission granted, Colonel," answered the president in a tone that made it quite clear she wanted and needed this man to speak his mind.

# 28

"With all due respect," began the colonel with a speech he had rehearsed and given in his own mind tens of times, "the belief that, once humans cut through the atmosphere into the vacuum of space, our flaws, greed, prejudices, and military ambition would be left behind is nothing more than some utopian crock of shit...pardon my language. And, in my opinion...a gross dereliction of duty."

Two of those at the table tsked in shock. As they did, Tim Shannon made eye contact with the man he had the pleasure of working with in the past and shot him a quick wink of encouragement.

"Since the dawn of our space program," continued Richards, "various presidents and members of Congress have gone out of their way to ensure that we did *not* have a military space program. Did not. While those actions may have appeased those who believed in the fairy tale that humanity's aggression and hate somehow magically stopped sixty miles above the planet, it did nothing to help protect the interests of our nation or her people. Worse than nothing, in fact."

"Now, just a minute," cut in Roger Cunningham, the current head of the Department of Homeland Security and a former senator. "I did not come here to be lectured by some colonel most of us have barely or never heard of."

"Pardon *me*, Roger," said the president with her voice now razor sharp. "Three nuclear weapons have just been detonated. Over a hundred thousand human beings are dead or dying. If you can't handle some tough language from an expert in the warfare we will soon have to engage in"—she paused to shoot a look of certitude at every single person sitting around the table before coming back to him—"then I honestly hope you will resign your position right this second so you can be replaced by someone totally focused on getting our planet's balls out of the vise now tightening around them."

At the same instant, Peter McNamara, Tim Shannon, and Bill Richards smiled in reflexive approval at the president's apt metaphor and lowered their heads in unison to try and hide their reactions.

As they did, Roger Cunningham's face turned bright red as he tried to backpedal out of the now embarrassing spot he had gotten himself into.

"Madam President," sputtered the director of Homeland Security. "I'm sorry. In no way—"

"Roger," said the president with a bit less steel in her voice. "Are you in or out? That's all I have time to hear."

"In," answered the patrician white-haired official.

"Great," answered the president, looking to take some of the sting away. "Because we surely need you."

Cunningham sheepishly nodded his head before beginning to examine the gleaming tabletop in minute detail.

"Colonel," implored the president as she looked toward Richards. "Please continue…as you see fit."

"Thank you, Madam President. In a nutshell, as the president was kind enough to mention, my paper focused on space warfare. More specifically, the response of the United States should we be attacked by an enemy operating from the moon. Now, to be sure, when I wrote the paper, I had the Russians and Chinese in mind…"

"But," interrupted the president, "you did include a very interesting hypothetical situation. One that General McNamara was insistent that I read immediately."

"Yes, Madam President," answered Richards as he slowed himself just a bit to organize his thoughts. "While I was at the Naval War College, I had a professor who himself had been a colonel serving at the Ballistic Missile Defense Organization at the Pentagon back in the day. He mentioned to me that, around 1990, when we were in high-level discussions with the then senior military leadership of the Soviet Union regarding the reduction of nuclear warheads, he and his team had met with two Russian generals. After the official business for the day was concluded, they arranged a private dinner for the generals. During the course of that dinner, there was a fair amount of alcohol flowing. Towards the end of the evening, the Soviet generals were feeling no pain and decided to volunteer two jaw-dropping bits of information which were ultimately… interconnected. The first general stated that, if the day finally came where the Soviet Union had to give up every single nuclear weapon and missile they had, they would still hide five from the world. The general then explained that, if it was discovered that in two days time a comet was about to hit the Earth and kill everyone on the planet, they would take those five warheads, attach them to the five remaining missiles, and launch them into Germany the day before. Such was the pain, suffering, and outright hate they still felt toward

Germany for the millions they lost at the hands of the Nazis during World War II."

While shocking in an academic way, it was a hypothetical situation that never came to pass. President Garcia only had ears for the next part of the story.

"And the *other* bit of jaw-dropping information?" asked the president as she arched her left eyebrow.

"According to my professor, the other Soviet general topped the first by revealing that, toward the very end of World War II when the Russians were just about to overrun the Peenemünde rocket base, one of their forward observation teams saw several rockets take off one after the other during a rainstorm at dusk. The rockets, the general insisted, were multiple sizes larger than the V-2. He followed that up by saying, 'I always wondered who was in those rockets and how many.'"

"How come I never heard of this," asked Secretary of Defense Mike Jensen.

"Yes, sir," answered Richards to his superior, and a man he respected immensely. "It's sort of been a bit of an urban myth within the military and our intelligence services for the last forty years or so. Because the obvious and expected reaction from anyone hearing something like this is to dismiss it out of hand as crazy and impossible, I suspect most were simply fearful to mention it to you. The professor I had who was privy to that conversation with the Soviet generals told me that while he was not inclined to dismiss the story, he was also afraid to talk about it fearing it would damage or even end his career. He said that, while the Soviet general was indeed drunk, there was something in his eyes that convinced my professor that, at the very least, he *believed* what he was saying to be true."

"So, you included that 'urban myth' in your paper," declared the president.

"Yes, Madam President. Part of it in a few paragraphs. More as a way to spice up the paper so those grading it wouldn't fall asleep as they evaluated my academic strategy to defend ourselves from an enemy encamped on the moon. That alone was already a stretch for some."

"And what, precisely," asked the president as she looked around the table to see everyone's attention riveted upon the colonel, "is that strategy?"

# 29

The door to the spider-looking lunar rover opened, and Ian Stewart and Venus Washington were lifted off their feet and dragged out of the vehicle and placed in the middle seat of what looked very much like an extended golf cart back on Earth.

As soon as they were both slammed into the seat, they were chained to a metal bar attached to the back of the seat in front of them. Just before one of the beings put a blindfold over his and Washington's eyes, Stewart saw another of the creatures drive up to the lunar rover in a small vehicle with a bed in the back like a pickup truck.

As soon as he did, one of the beings in the lunar rover picked up Robert Marshall's body and threw it in the bed of the small truck, where it grotesquely bounced around for several seconds in the low lunar gravity before finally settling in a twisted, lifeless heap.

No sooner did that happen than the blindfold enveloped Stewart in darkness and the cart they sat upon jerked forward in movement.

Ian Stewart had never been a fatalist. Since he was a small boy, he had always been able to figure things out. Always able to solve puzzles. Always able to arrive at the proper conclusion or answer long before everyone else. While he was not a religious person, per se, he was very spiritual. He did believe in the same god for all people, and he did believe that God had blessed him with a very good mind.

A gift he never tried to take for granted and often used to help others around him.

But now, the gift seemed like a curse.

First, because as his mind tried to process the impossible, there were still holes he could not fill. Answers he could not come up with. Images he could not square with the reality projected by life on Earth.

From the second he looked out the window of their lunar lander and saw the vehicle with the Nazi swastika emblazoned on the front, his gift of a mind could only function in spurts between long spells of fear, confusion, and growing dread.

Although he had become a celebrated test pilot and fighter pilot for the Air Force, he had never seen combat. Never.

Like many men and women in the military or on various police forces, he believed—and desperately hoped—that if the time came and he was forced into a combat situation, his training would kick in and he would perform as expected.

But…that test never came, so the question was never answered.

Most especially within his own mind.

Stewart was under no illusions as to why he had been picked as the commander for the first American lunar landing since 1972. It was *because* of his first-rate mind. Because he was technically a flawless pilot. Because, during endless simulations on Earth, he handled the lunar lander better than any other pilot-astronaut at NASA. And finally, he was picked because the entire leadership of NASA was convinced that he was the best problem solver in the bunch.

The best.

Under the blackness of the blindfold and as the cart they were chained to continued down what seemed to be an endless roadway or corridor, Stewart shook his head in disgust at NASA's clearly false faith in him.

His great mind, his technical expertise, and his perfect simulation scores could not problem-solve his ass out of this nightmare.

Either some hallucinogenic drug had seeped into the lunar lander upon touchdown on the moon, or the eight-foot humanoids in black space suits and the formal dress of the monstrous Gestapo who had taken them prisoner were real.

Homicidally real.

Stewart's mind was functioning well enough to realize—and accept—that the beings were not some drug-induced illusion.

Robert Marshall *had* been murdered. Venus Washington might soon be sexually violated, and he most likely would be tortured.

That's the reality his "gifted" mind had now settled upon.

Fatalism now seemed like the only faith to follow.

Should he get his mind right for the inevitable and simply let go like one trapped underwater who can no longer hold his breath, or should he fight until that very last breath is exhausted in the vain hope that an air pocket or even an escape was seconds away?

Suddenly, what he saw next hit his last exposed nerve and blew up the comfort zone of fatalism that his mind was all but finished constructing. It was as if a spoonful of salt had been smeared into an open wound.

His reaction was visceral.

He would *fight*.

He would claw, he would bite, he would kick, and he would scream until that last breath was taken from him.

He had instantly never felt so at peace, or his mind and body strengthen as they did, as when he saw the trigger to that emotion.

The cart had stopped. The chains taken off him and Venus.

They were violently pulled from their seat and led up a small staircase. They were then pushed and pulled across a floor until just as suddenly stopped in their tracks.

Stewart had both of his arms jerked upward and then wrapped around what felt like a metal pole of some kind. As his hands were being re-chained, he began to hear it.

It was a murmur at first. Growing with each millisecond into an unnatural hum that seemed to reverberate off some far-away walls and intensify.

As Venus was being chained, the hum became guttural and strangely...*perverse.*

At that instant, Venus screamed out in terror and slumped to the floor unconscious.

As soon as she did, the blindfold was ripped off Stewart's face and he saw the cause of Washington's terror and...the source of the hum.

They were both chained to a pole in the center of some kind of large stage. A stage that looked down upon a massive arena.

An arena that was filled with at least ten thousand super-humanoid Nazis standing at attention in perfect unison with multiple Nazi flags hanging from the ceiling above them.

Ten thousand.

As Stewart saw them, the very first thought that flashed in his mind was the scene from the original *Planet of the Apes* movie where the Charlton Heston and Nova characters were put on display before the ape generals.

Revulsion at the obscenity of the sight almost caused him to vomit.

One thought, and one *oath* to himself, burst to the forefront of Stewart's mind: *No fuckin' way this Nazi scum touch my family or anyone else on Earth. No way.*

As that thought was cementing itself to his mind, a door at the side of the stage opened and eight heavily armed humanoids walked out.

As soon as they did, the ten thousand beings on the floor of the arena snapped their right arms in perfect uniformity and screamed out: "Sieg Heil!"

As the echoes of the scream filled the cavernous arena, Stewart tried to comprehend what was happening. Then, it dawned on him.

The eight heavily armed storm troopers were a protective security detail. They were *not* the catalyst for the Nazi salute.

As Stewart looked at the storm troopers approaching him—all closer to nine feet tall and four hundred pounds of pure muscle—he caught a glimpse of a brown-uniformed figure in the middle of them.

*This* was the being they were protecting and the one who elicited the roar of prideful loyalty and…worship.

Between the massive arms, chests, and weapons advancing closer, Stewart flicked his eyes repeatedly back and forth while squinting to get a clear look at the smaller figure dwarfed and hidden among the bubble of evil.

And then, for one split second he had it. He could see the being. And when he did, time, and his very mind, stood still. Locked in place by the insanity that had been dialed up beyond any and all human comprehension.

# 30

"My strategy," answered Richards in grateful appreciation of the confidence the president of the United States was affording him, "is to first assume the very worst."

The president closed her eyes for a moment, and her mind's eye flashed her the unfathomable pictures of the death and destruction in Russia.

"That is the only assumption I am working from, Colonel," said the president as her eyes snapped back open from the horror of the images.

Richards nodded. "Yes, ma'am. If we work from that assumption, then in many ways it really doesn't matter who is up on the moon. Russians, Chinese, Nazis, Martians. It does not matter. We—meaning most especially the United States—are for the time being pretty much fu…uh…sorry…in a really bad place. As you know—and have been briefed—Madam President, there is no nation on Earth more dependent upon its satellites in low and geosynchronous orbit for its national and economic security than us. At the

Space Corps, we war-gamed that reality a number of times in a number of ways. Focusing at the time primarily on the People's Republic of China and their military space program combined with their continuous and aggressive targeting of our satellites, we came to the conclusion that they could declare...and *achieve*...total victory without a shot or a missile being fired. Once they took out all of our satellites, we would be totally blind and unable to defend ourselves. Knowing that—and with all due respect, Madam President—the leadership of China would simply have to dial up the president of the United States in the Oval Office and then dictate the terms of our total and unconditional surrender. Switch out the Chinese for the Nazis and you get the same result. Check that. A clearly more brutal result."

"Pardon me, Colonel," interrupted FBI Director Bentley, "but that sounds somewhat far-fetched."

"It's not," corrected Secretary of Defense Jensen. "We've *all* war-gamed it at one time or another, and it was something that kept us up at night. Hence, the creation of the Space Corps. Unfortunately," continued Jensen as he looked over at Roger Cunningham, then at Bentley, before settling on the president, "because of partisan politics, Congress kept delaying and delaying the proper funding of the Space Corps. Beyond that, and as you know, Carolina..."

It still bothered a few at the table that Jensen could, first, get away with calling the president by her first name, second, that she would allow it, and last, that it still seemed much less respectful than the title bestowed upon her by the voters.

"...there is a tendency for certain presidents to roll back or outright cancel programs started by previous presidents. Especially if they came from the opposing party."

This time, Vice President Antonio Deluca—the former governor of Florida—raised his voice in protest.

"Now just a second, Mike," began the vice president in defense of his party and his running mate.

"Stop," spoke up Carolina Garcia with her hand in the air. "First, Mike is correct and we all know it. Next, given our dire predicament I declare that, from here on out, there will be a moratorium on *any and all* partisan politics and the defense of such. *If* we somehow survive all of this, we should and must examine the great damage done to our nation time and time again when a new president and a new Congress roll into power and cancel effective and needed programs or policies *only* because the other party offered them up. But…that's a big 'if.' Right now, I just want to get back to the briefing from Colonel Richards."

President Garcia turned to look at the colonel again with a slight glint of resigned bemusement in her dark brown eyes.

"So, Colonel," she asked as she lifted her coffee cup. "What is the 'secret sauce' that was the by-product of your flight-of-imagination school paper all those years ago?"

When finished with the question, she took a quick sip of her coffee and made the tiniest face of disappointment noticing it had gone cold.

Before Richards could answer, Tim Shannon pushed his chair back, walked to the back of the room, poured a fresh cup of hot coffee, and brought it back along with the sugar and cream. He then silently put all before the president.

As he did, the president caressed the back of his hand in loving gratitude.

While Bentley, Sun, and now Cunningham made barely concealed faces of disapproval at the first open confirmation of the romance between the president and the head of NASA, others in the room were deeply touched and honestly happy for the president. Most especially McNamara, Jensen, and Richards. Three individuals who had seen combat, knew the horror that lay before them all, and had been sustained and comforted in the past by the love and support of a spouse or a soul mate.

Combined, the three veterans had over seventy years of military service. In their opinion, Carolina Garcia was the best commander in chief they had ever served under.

Because of her very tough childhood and upbringing, they were well aware she had never lost sight of how truly hard life was for the majority of people in both the United States and, indeed, the world. Like the members of the Secret Service detail that protected her, Garcia truly understood the sacrifice being made by those who volunteered to serve in the military, and she considered their lives precious.

One had to make the case beyond a shadow of a doubt to her that members of the United States military should be put in harm's way in the best interests of the country. If not, she would not authorize the deployment of even one soldier, sailor, or airman. It truly pained Carolina Garcia to know that she personally had to approve sending young Americans into a theater of combat.

If such a decision went bad, the loss of innocent life would settle its heavy and haunting weight upon her shoulders for the rest of her life.

That said, she was far from too sensitive or naïve not to understand that, at certain times, the military force of the United States had to be called upon to protect the nation and her people.

If and when those times reared their ugly head, she was more than prepared to authorize the action.

But once she made such a decision, she then personally lobbied to make sure overwhelming force and the best chance for victory accompanied the military into the coming battle.

Back in the day, that strategy became known as "the Colin Powell Doctrine," and she was a firm believer in the wisdom and experience that went into that unofficial commandment.

Everyone from the SecDef to the Joint Chiefs of Staff to the rank-and-file troops not only knew that, but revered her because of it.

She had their backs. Period.

Richards turned to look at Shannon, who was once again assuming his chair, and slightly nodded his head at the gesture of caring and compassion. He then turned back to face the president and waited for her to fix her coffee and take a now *hot* sip.

"Madam President. I'd fight."

Richards widened his own eyes and tilted his head just a bit in self-deprecating acknowledgment of his proffered advice that a Pentagon buddy used to laughingly label "a blinding flash of the obvious."

As a few of the senior leadership in the Situation Room were no doubt saying "duh" to themselves, Richards went on.

"Fight not only in the sense of battle and war, but *much* more importantly, the kind of fight that at least *our* nation can handle better than any other on Earth...and hopefully, the moon. That being a logistics and industrial battle. If we have enough time before our hand is forced and we are attacked again here on Earth...and I believe we *will*...then—"

"Wait, Colonel," jumped in the president. "Why do you think we will have more time before they hit Earth again?"

Richards swiveled his high-back black office chair to better face the president.

"On the flight out here, I read the background regarding the three nuclear attacks they launched. At least, the background emailed to me at that time. I found it very curious that the Nazis— or whatever they truly are up there—used reentry spacecraft from China, Russia, and us as the delivery vehicles to hit us with their nuclear weapons. Now, it could have been that they were simply trying to be clever. Or, it could be that their own technology or spacecraft are not advanced enough to, first, survive a journey back down through our atmosphere and the five thousand or so degrees of heat that will envelope the reentry vehicle, and second, even if they could survive the reentry, that they are not good enough to hit a city or military installation they want to target."

"And *what*, Colonel," asked the president—who generally subscribed to the rule offered up to first-year law students to *never* ask a question you did not already know or suspect the answer to—"is the answer you came up with for your very own riddle?"

# 31

Helmut Brandt, the forty-one-year-old chancellor of Germany, sat at his desk with his head buried in his hands and wept silently to himself.

As he did, tears and the mucus building up in his nose fell freely upon the top-secret report lying before him on the desk. A report that had been delivered minutes earlier by the head of the Bundesnachrichtendienst, his nation's Federal Intelligence Service.

The report was dated May 10, 1945.

In the eighty-four years since the report was hastily typed out, its white pages had yellowed substantially within the still bright red binder of the Third Reich that held it.

Unfortunately for Chancellor Brandt, the mind-altering words contained within the report were all too easy to read...if not comprehend and process.

As the chancellor was just told by his intelligence chief, the report had been written in the final days of the war by an anonymous officer who hid in a storage closet from a mass execution at the Peenemünde rocket base and then escaped just before Russian troops overran the facility.

While it appeared the anonymous officer may have been a lower-ranking intelligence official, he was also one, as declared in the report, who felt Hitler was "a madman who was sabotaging the world for decades and even centuries to come, with time bombs he had strategically hidden."

The report outlined "the most ambitious time bomb of all." One that would allow the most fanatical followers of Hitler to not only flee the grasp—and justice—of anyone on Earth but give them the time needed to breed, flourish, and prepare…for *revenge*.

The report ended up in a box of hundreds of other documents that managed to elude discovery by the Russians and the Americans in the weeks and months following the end of the war.

The box was not opened again until 1949, during the first year of Chancellor Konrad Adenauer's administration.

The box, and all in it, was sent directly to Adenauer's chief of intelligence at the time. A man who then found the fantastical report buried within a box of other documents, read it, and instantly *knew* it to be true.

He had made a unilateral decision right on the spot. No one but himself and those who would follow him as the head of intelligence during the coming years and decades would ever see the report.

No one. *Ever.*

He very logically assumed—and literally paused to pray after reading the report—that no group could possibly survive such a crazy and hazardous journey. And if they did, they would soon die a horrible death upon that barren, airless, and hostile landscape.

With that assumption and prayer in mind, the report was passed along *only* to the next head of the Federal Intelligence Service. Each time, with but *one line of instruction.* That being that if "irrefutable proof ever emerged" that the assumption of failure was wrong and "the darkest of evil" ever known to humanity *had* reconstituted itself on that alien world, then the most top-secret report in the history of Germany should be immediately given to the nation's current chancellor.

The head of the Bundesnachrichtendienst considered three nuclear explosions and one hundred thousand dead Russians to be "irrefutable proof." That, combined with the top-secret information he had recently been given.

As the cliché has always accurately predicted, nothing becomes obsolete faster than a "military secret."

Aside from the nuclear explosions immediately known to the world, a report and video from NASA had been shared with the National Security Council at the White House. A report naturally hidden from the world.

Or so…the White House believed.

For entirely self-serving reasons, a CIA operative detailed to the NSC then back-channeled the pertinent hair-raising details of the report and video to his wife, who was an executive for a Silicon Valley start-up and was meeting with venture capitalists in Berlin.

German intelligence immediately trapped the leak of ultra-top-secret information and brought it to the attention of the head of the Bundesnachrichtendienst.

Within seconds of being told of the intelligence leak from the White House, the head of the Bundesnachrichtendienst opened the safe in his wall, pulled out the decades-hidden report, scanned it one more time, closed his safe, and personally walked the binder to the chancellor's office.

\* \* \*

CHANCELLOR BRANDT GRABBED a couple of tissues from the pop-up box on his desk and slowly wiped his eyes, nose, and then the pages of the report stained by his unleashed sadness and misery.

Over eight decades after the end of World War II and some—
*too many*—still held the people of *today's* Germany responsible for
the worst and most horrific mass killing in the history of the world.

*The Holocaust.*

Two words that not only titled the greatest crime against
humanity, but haunted most of the citizens of Germany today
with thoughts of shame, remorse, and the never-ending hope for
forgiveness.

Forgiveness for something they, their parents, and even their
grandparents had nothing to do with. Nothing.

The chancellor knew—and logic dictated—that at some point,
blame would no longer be assigned to men, women, and children
born decades, and now almost a century, after that crime against
humanity.

Crimes history recorded, which were also carried out by the
Egyptians, the Romans, and the Greeks two-to-six thousand years
before. Truly horrible crimes no longer spot-welded to the current
inhabitants of those nations.

Innocent people who no longer felt the wrath of blame. Innocent people who no longer had fingers of guilt by association
pointed at them. Innocent people finally allowed to go on with their
lives without a cloak of shame being permanently attached to their
shoulders at birth.

To be fair, the chancellor also mentally acknowledged that fewer
and fewer people were associating the people of today's Germany
with its dark past.

At least...they *had* been.

*But now*, he thought. *But now...this...this...our worst nightmare
realized. The world will once again come to blame us...once again,
come to hate us...once again seek to punish us....*

An uncontrollable fit of sobbing hit the German chancellor
once more. After a minute or so, he was able to get his breathing

back under control. After using several more tissues to clean his face, he reached for the phone on his desk and dialed a private phone number.

A female voice answered the call after the second ring. She was the chancellor of Austria.

"Greta," stated the German chancellor with no introduction and zero pleasantries. "We need to assemble an army. Now. Today. The very best of our best. An army that will atone for sins associated with our past, speak to our honor of today, and help to vanquish an evil which will not die."

# 32

Ian Stewart's grandfather had always considered himself to be a bit of an amateur historian. Most especially when it came to military history.

At eighteen years of age and right after graduation from high school, George McNeil had volunteered to enlist in the United States Army. While it seemed like a selfless act, McNeil knew it was anything but. His draft number was six, which meant the military was going to come for him whether he liked it or not.

His choices were then boiled down to: enlist and at least control a tiny portion of his own fate, or flee to Canada as some of his classmates and friends who opposed the war in Vietnam had done.

Though McNeil felt the undeclared "war" was unjust and not in the best interests of the United States, he was also not one for fleeing his country.

He enlisted, volunteered, and was eventually chosen for Special Forces, and served two tours of heavy-duty combat in Vietnam. He returned to the United States disgusted by the needless waste of local and US military life, joined the Postal Service, had a family, retired with a pension, and then made it his hobby…and *business*… to understand past wars and what made *any* of them worth the loss of thousands to millions of innocent lives.

Before he passed at eighty-seven years of age, he had accumulated one of the best military history libraries—books, videos, and DVDs—this side of the Library of Congress.

Stewart was introduced to this amazing collection at an early age by his doting grandfather, who hoped to cultivate his grandson's obvious streak of intellectual curiosity.

One of the DVD collections he remembered watching—at first, to see the aircraft of the time—was a six-volume set titled, *World War II in Color.*

Seeing the carnage of war in living color was not something a twelve-year-old should have been witnessing. Young Stewart instantly learned to hit the fast-forward button on the old VCR-DVD player while squinting his eyes when those disturbing scenes popped up on the screen.

As much as he was repulsed and close to physically sickened by the footage of human beings taking the lives of other human beings in battle for "God and country," he was just as fascinated with it as he was by the historical video of a nondescript little man who always seemed to keep himself in an eccentric bubble of solitude slightly away from all others when he walked, talked, or gave orders.

The man on the screen came across as weak, insecure, guarded, paranoid, but strangely—and even hyperactively—creative.

His eyes were always darting about in equal amounts of predator and prey.

Young Ian had seen such a person before.

That person being a homeless man of about fifty who lived by himself in a self-built shack in the woods not too far from the middle school Ian attended at the time.

Every once in a while, Ian and his eighth-grade friends would see the man loitering near the town's little strip mall. People said he had once been a professor at Harvard but lost his mind when he had lost his family in a car accident. Others said he was simply an alcoholic prone to fits of irrational behavior best to be left alone.

While Ian never got too close to the homeless man, he did watch him from time to time from the front window of the local sub shop.

He watched him because he had *seen* that man before. The stooped shoulders, the darting eyes, the odd and unkempt hairstyle, the scribbled drawings and equations, and the constant fear of real human interaction.

Young Ian would stare and then stare some more until it finally dawned on him where he had seen the man before.

He was the *featured figure* in his grandfather's World War II collection.

He was the insane loser and megalomaniac responsible for the deaths of tens of millions of people.

The homeless guy near the strip mall was a three-dimensional Rorschach image of the most reviled man in history:

*Adolf Hitler.*

A man young Ian Stewart had seen repeatedly while watching his grandfather's DVDs.

A man…that *exact* man…who was *now* standing hidden and protected by the nine-foot-tall storm troopers on a stage, in some massive hall, within some kind of lunar colony hidden deep within a mountain range at the South Pole of the moon.

Ian Stewart took one more look at the feeble little man in the brown uniform, closed his eyes, and proceeded to vomit all over the stage before he was knocked unconscious by one of his captors.

# 33

"Madam President," began Richards in answer to her question. "Based only upon my gut feelings and instinct, I believe we forced their hand a little with the almost simultaneous lunar landings by us and the Chinese. And, no matter if we did or not, I feel that it's critical to believe that they have the ability to monitor our transmissions and communications here on Earth. An ability they have most likely had for years. If we use that assumption as a foundation of understanding, then it would follow that they have been well aware that we, the Chinese, the Russians, and various private enterprises are coming to the moon...to stay. They—and for planning purposes, I will refer to them as Nazis—don't have to be told of the strategic importance of the moon. After having lived there for over eight decades, they would have realized—and capitalized upon—its military, economic, and scientific advantages. Advantages they would never agree to share but clearly will defend at all costs. Did we accelerate a military strategy or campaign they may have already had in mind? Again, it's only my instinct, but I believe so."

President Garcia shifted her eyes to look quickly at Peter McNamara and then Tim Shannon. Both men subtly nodded their heads at Richards' gut assumption.

"Because," the president said as she trained her eyes back on the colonel, "they used our own spacecraft to deliver their nuclear warheads."

"Yes. In part. Again, they could have been just using our own spacecraft as a perverse way to amuse themselves, but I don't believe so. Ultimately, if we go back to our base strategy of always assuming the worst with this enemy, then in the short run, it does not matter. Whether they were ready or not, they announced themselves to the planet Earth in the most horrific of ways. That said, if they did use our spacecraft because they don't yet have the capability to hit a target on Earth with their own vehicles, then we might have a gift of time unintentionally built into the equation."

"And what do you propose we do with that gift of time, Colonel? If there is indeed one."

"Prepare. While they may or may not have the ability to reenter Earth's atmosphere to attack us on the ground, they do have the ability to take out all of our satellites and blind us."

Richards had given this one a great deal of thought and only needed buy-in from one person: President Garcia.

"Not only must our nation instantly drop everything we are doing in the public and private sectors to engage in the most critically important military, industrial, and logistical Marshall Plan of all time," continued Richards as he shed the last of his nervousness, "we must also enlist any and all nations on Earth capable of contributing to the same. That means *everybody*. Not just the Russians, the Chinese, or the G-8 nations. But everyone. Every hemisphere, every ideology, every language, every faith, everyone. If they can contribute anything to this fight, they are in. They *must* be in."

"I am very happy to hear you say that, Colonel," acknowledged the president with just the briefest of smiles. "I had come to the exact same conclusion. In this job, presidents usually don't have a great deal of spare time to themselves. In the past, some have worked harder than others. Some, not so much. As corny and naïve as it may sound to some, I ran for this office primarily because I wanted to see if I could make a positive difference for our fellow citizens who never get a seat at the various power tables in our nation. Because of that, I honestly felt that in my 'spare' time, it was my duty to learn as much about my predecessors as possible. Starting with George Washington. I don't read novels. I don't watch reality television. I don't give a rat's ass what the latest 'Housewife of Hedonism' is doing. I read and watch the words of those in this job before me. That *is* my spare time. I take in the good and most productive words and the bad and most partisan rubbish. With all of that in mind, I came across some truly relevant and timely words. During his second term in office, President Ronald Reagan said something, Colonel, which very much spoke to our need for planetary unity now. In 1987, during an address before the United Nations General Assembly, President Reagan said: 'I occasionally think how quickly our differences worldwide would vanish if we were facing an alien threat from outside of this world.'

"Naturally, President Reagan's prescient words were met with ridicule and insult by the elites and intellectual and partisan snobs of the time.

"Interestingly enough, almost thirty years later while appearing on a late-night program, former president Bill Clinton echoed the words of Reagan and his hypothetical attack from an alien threat by saying: 'It may be the only way to unite this increasingly divided world of ours.' Well…for *every* intent and purpose, the Nazi force on the moon *is* that alien threat from another world, and for the sake of humanity now, it *better* unite us."

* * *

"Amen," said Richards with a smile of his own.

The president looked down at her watch and then back up at Richards and those gathered.

"Colonel. At this point, give me the thumbnail sketch. As we just agreed, I have a great many calls to make. Starting with another secure teleconference any second with the leaders of Russia and China."

"Yes, Madam President. Okay, so the elevator pitch, and going back to that worst-case scenario, we need to prepare ourselves immediately for the loss of every satellite we have. Phones, GPS, television, banking, airlines, hospital records, everything. Although we, the Russians, the Chinese, and others war-game that possibility from time to time, we must actually prepare for it…*now*. Like all of us, I have lived and prospered through and thanks to technology, but I have always been aware that it's also very much like a Venus flytrap enticing us closer and closer with its tempting ease of 'but a push of a button' or a voice command until it traps and kills all who become fat and lazy."

"Valid point, Colonel," said the president. "One that I have pondered and actually worried about off and on for years. Most especially since assuming this job. I have often thought that, very much like the metaphor of 'in the land of the blind, a one-eyed man is king,' in today's world—ultra-dependent upon technology for our very survival—a town, city, or even small country that went totally back to paper records, landlines, and VHF and UHF transmissions could one day conquer and rule over those soon blind."

"Precisely," answered Richards, pleased with her response. "And it is *exactly* the example you just cited that we have to begin to replicate now. Today. We are going to need a way to talk to each other. To ask questions. To communicate orders. To build spacecraft and weapons. To launch attacks. To create electricity with old-school hidden and portable generators. With that need and urgency in mind, we have to reach out to every facet of corporate America and its government counterparts that keep exponentially improving our technology, robotics, and artificial intelligence, and order them to *stop everything* and *go back in time* to create strategically placed pockets of 1960's communications and landlines in order to speak to each other and sustain us during the coming attacks and...in my forecast...war."

# 34

When Stewart came to, he found his head resting in a pool of his own vomit on the floor of the stage, looking up at two legs encased in a space suit. After another few seconds, he realized that the legs belonged to Venus Washington.

Stewart turned his bruised and bleeding head slightly to see that, while she was once again awake and now standing, she was clutching the pole they were chained to with both hands and with her eyes tightly shut.

As she came into focus, Stewart next became aware of a voice reverberating somewhere close at hand. A voice that continually switched from shrill, to monotone, to screaming, to cracking like a pubescent teenage boy. Fearful of being struck yet again by one of the lunar monstrosities towering near him, Stewart ever so slowly tilted his head toward the direction of the screeching voice.

His eyes soon came to rest upon…*Adolf Hitler.*

The living, breathing, talking *exact* reincarnation of *der Führer* was standing at a podium twenty feet from him, squealing out some seemingly fanatical remarks to the cheering throng of ten thousand storm troopers assembled in the hall.

A performance Stewart had watched multiple times on a television at his grandfather's home some two decades before was now being played out live before him by some wildly gesticulating atrocity of creation.

How?

Stewart's mind had now fully accepted that what was happening to him and all around him was real. No matter how bizarre it was, or would get.

The darker survivalist corner of his mind was now demanding that he ruthlessly stomp out any and all questions regarding how and why.

It *is* as it seems was the new and *only* reality.

With that part of his brain finally activated and engaged, Stewart truly did feel that growing sense of inner peace and strength. While he knew he would most likely still be killed in the most gruesome of ways, he was grateful that his mind was clearing and at least attempting to process not only his new and savage reality, but actually take it all in and search for any hint of a weakness or escape.

As Stewart turned his eyes to observe the hall of storm troopers who all seemed to be in a trance of complete adulation and even worship, he just as quickly realized that "escape" was a stupid and wasted thought.

Accepting that conclusion, that dark corner of his mind that controlled his "go fuck yourself" instincts instantly switched gears.

Fueled by the adrenaline now seeping into it, that part of his brain went to the next item on its "let's get crazy" list.

As the escape option was clearly dead on arrival, what was left?

Resistance for pride's sake?

Sabotage something?

What?

Suddenly, Stewart's counterintuitively calm mind jumped all the way up to item number one on the "bat-shit crazy" list.

*What if,* Stewart began to ask himself with the building excitement of a condemned prisoner with nothing left to lose, *I go out in that proverbial 'blaze of glory' by killing that abhorrent plague of debauchery standing at the podium before they kill me?*

As if on cue, Lunar Hitler turned toward him and Venus and began pointing and wildly waving his arms about as spittle flew out of his mouth propelled by the increase in deranged screaming.

As the thousands of storm troopers grunted out their apelike noises of approval, Stewart's attention was temporarily diverted as his eyes momentarily focused on one huge drop of saliva that was cascading to the floor of the stage between Lunar Hitler and himself and Venus.

Because of that split-second "shiny object" distraction of the mind, Stewart's gaze happened to fall upon the right side of the stage.

And there, behind a curtain shielded from all in the audience, was the commander of the Nazi force who had taken him and Venus prisoner.

A commander who seemed to be trying to get the attention of the Lunar Hitler without anyone else being the wiser. A commander who—contrary to the perceived reality—came across as now visibly angry with the person who was surely his boss—and quite likely a deity of some type.

Finally, the frail five-foot, eight-inch man at the podium noticed the eight-foot-plus slab of muscular granite off to the side of the stage. When he did, the military commander angrily pointed toward the prisoners and then his own mouth. He repeated the gesture three times rapidly in succession, as if to remind the speaker of something.

Then, just as quickly averting his eyes and attention from the military commander, Lunar Hitler nodded his head and suddenly walked directly toward Stewart and Washington while all the while still screaming out his diatribe in German to the storm troopers.

When he was but two feet away, Lunar Hitler stopped, bent down, and spit in Stewart's face. He then stood straight up, turned, and did the same in Washington's face.

Satisfied with his performance, Lunar Hitler then turned on his heel in a practiced fashion and walked back to the podium to escalating screams of approval from the thousands of Nazis on the floor of the hall.

As he did, Stewart realized that he just missed his chance to "go out in a blaze of glory." Surely, he could have wrapped his legs around the little man and snapped his neck with his chained hands before the monsters could kill him.

But he didn't.

No.

Instead, his mind and body froze as he tried to comprehend the interaction he had just inadvertently witnessed.

As a glob of Lunar Hitler's spit oozed down the side of his nose and dripped onto the cold floor of the stage, Stewart shifted his eyes back to look at the military commander. A being who now had the satisfied look of someone who had just put an underling in his place.

Stewart shifted his eyes once again to focus on Lunar Hitler. As he screamed out the final minutes of his speech, Stewart came to the realization that there was nothing "deranged" about it.

Nothing at all.

It was planned theatrics that spoke to a much more ominous purpose and…fate.

# 35

Minutes after the world learned of the nuclear attack in Russia that killed tens of thousands of people, Operation Atlantis was activated.

Almost ten years earlier to the day, four of the world's wealthiest billionaires—each one worth over $50 billion—had met in Aspen, Colorado, for potentially the most important and certainly most confidential meeting of their lives.

Two of the billionaires were from the United States, one from Russia, and the last from the United Kingdom.

At the time of the first meeting, all were under the age of fifty and each had independently been spending tens of millions of dollars on private doctors and unlicensed clinics around the world in search of some form of "immortality."

Because of their out-of-control egos, sycophantic adulation of staff, and various politicians—who, respectively, only wanted to pay the bills or get reelected—and delusional and unstable minds from the cocktail of drugs each was already regularly taking in an attempt to cheat death, they had no problem convincing themselves that they were *indispensable* to the world and that therefore, "It is our responsibility to the unwashed masses to try and live at least centuries more so we can lead and guide those unfortunate cretins."

At that first meeting, all had entered into a pact. Each would use an equal amount of their fortunes to build a bunker that would sustain them and as many as two thousand people for upward of a decade without the need for resupply.

But not just any "bunker." It would be the most luxurious complex...*never* known.

Under the guise of "protecting the world's oceans," the project was initiated two years later. Six months after that, the perfect site had been selected. It was a natural cave that extended almost a mile into a ridge of solid rock one hundred miles to the east of Veracruz, Mexico.

A ridge eight hundred feet *below* the surface of the Gulf of Mexico.

Under the cover of their charity, while continually paying or buying off any curious government officials or members of the media, the self-absorbed billionaires succeeded in building what amounted to a totally self-sustaining, 1,000-foot-long, 150-foot-high-and-wide, 5-inch-thick airtight steel tube capable of housing those...like them.

It was assembled piece-by-piece within the bowels of a massive container ship. Once complete, it was lowered via ballast—much like a submarine—to the mouth of the underwater cave one thousand feet below the ocean and then very slowly and very carefully inserted into the opening.

The ridge that held the natural cave provided three hundred feet of solid rock all around as protection. At the mouth of the opening, a blast door of ten-foot-thick steel was installed. A door that slid to the side to provide access to the docking port and multi-chamber airlock that led to the facility.

On the inside, it looked very much like a high-end cruise ship.

It contained restaurants, coffee shops, a movie theater, a spa and gym, a medical facility staffed by a spectrum of the best doctors, a general store, and much more.

The complex distilled over twenty thousand gallons of fresh water per day from the sea, made its own oxygen, and was powered by three small nuclear reactors built to last at least a quarter of a century.

Each of the four billionaires had a private three-thousand-square-foot suite in the facility they had designated the "New Atlantis," but which was instantly and secretly nicknamed "the Cigar" by the construction crew and staff.

Aside from their private suites, each of the billionaires had access to two of the five hundred cabins reserved for their invited guests and staff. Those cabins were for the mistresses they brought with them, as well as the ones they planned to groom during their lengthy stay.

Along with the billionaires, their families, their mistresses, invited guests, and the staff was a highly experienced twenty-five-person security team. Each member of the team had been a special operator in his or her home country, and each had served in multiple combat operations.

Five members of the team were on site *only* to protect the four billionaires. Period.

The remaining twenty were there to protect the facility.

In addition to every small and medium weapon and armament known to humanity at the time, this team also had a very special toy at its disposal—a one-fourth-scale model of a Russian hunter-killer submarine that the Russian billionaire had commissioned and built upon agreeing to help fund and live in the complex.

A submarine equipped with conventional and nuclear-tipped torpedoes.

Beyond that was a much smaller secondary docking port known only to the four billionaires and their security team. A docking port with another private submarine attached to ensure their escape should the main entrance be damaged or the facility come under attack from the outside…or even in the event of a potential mutiny from within the complex.

Once inside, the billionaires would not be blind to what was happening above them in the world. Far from it.

They had dedicated landlines installed in the facility that led to several stations strategically hidden on the surface and equipped with the best and most stealthy communications and video technology.

All monitored 24/7 in a control room of their New Atlantis.

Should the situation above worsen *or* get better, they would know it in real time and act accordingly.

At the moment, to the four billionaires' way of thinking, it could not be worse. The nuclear bomb detonated in Russia was all the encouragement they needed.

Minutes after learning the details of that deadly event, they activated a secret code sent around the world to the "Designated Survivors" each of the four had personally handpicked.

Within seventy-two hours of the signal being sent, approximately 1,400 people had arrived via private jets to the airport in Veracruz. Once there, they were transported to hotels near the harbor. Within five hours of arriving at the harbor, all 1,400 boarded a privately chartered cruise ship that then set sail in the dead of night to rendezvous with the container vessel that was readying three large submersibles to lower the guests to their new home inside a cave at the bottom of the Gulf of Mexico.

If the end of the world were coming, the four billionaires were now ready and in place to ride it out.

Or, at least…so they believed.

# 36

Before Colonel Richards could continue with his briefing, the president's personal aide stepped into the Situation Room, walked up to Carolina Garcia, and whispered in her ear.

The president nodded her head and then instinctively looked toward Tim Shannon before turning back to look at Colonel Richards.

"Colonel," began the president. "I apologize for the interruption. The presidents of Russia and China are ready for our teleconference. At this point, I'd rather keep this particular conversation as private as possible. President Medvedev is already on edge and stressed to the breaking point. Aside from that, President Li is notoriously paranoid of staff. Even his own. For those reasons, I'd ask that only the vice president and General McNamara stay with me for this call. Once it has been concluded, we can all regather to debrief."

All but those three stood, nodded at the president, and began to exit the room.

When he was just outside the doorway, Secretary of Defense Jensen turned to corral Richards and Shannon.

"Mind if I buy you guys a drink in private?"

Both men agreed, and Jensen led them about twenty feet away until they were standing at the entrance to the White House Mess, a private restaurant run by the United States Navy reserved exclusively for senior staff and invited guests.

Jensen was greeted at the podium leading down to the mess by the maître d'. The man shook Jensen's hand and then walked them down the few steps to the entrance of the mess.

The maître d' was going to point out the model of the USS *Constitution* and the 1790 original mess gong from that historic ship to Jensen's guests but thought better of it given the look of urgency in the SecDef's eyes.

As soon as they stood in the doorway, Jensen pointed to a table in the back partially hidden by a wood-paneled post.

Since the room had already been cleared out in anticipation of those from the Situation Room being in need of it, Jensen did not have to worry about privacy. That said, he opted for caution just in case some of the others were to stroll in.

No sooner had the three of them been seated than a female Filipino Navy steward walked over to greet them and take their drink order.

Jensen and Richards both opted for yet another coffee.

Tim Shannon ordered a large Coke with a side of fries.

After the steward left, the SecDef looked over at Shannon and laughed.

"A large Coke and a side of fries. What are you…like twelve now?"

"Hey," answered Shannon with a small laugh. "It's comfort food."

"I see," said Jensen as he powered down to a smile. "And maybe the president doesn't like to see you eat that shit in front of her."

"Maybe," offered Shannon. "President or not, when we are alone, she does work sometimes at making me...a better and healthier me."

"We'd be in big trouble if they didn't," said Richards. "No way can we function in civilized society on our own. At least not me."

"Roger that," declared Jensen.

Richards then leaned over and tapped Shannon on the shoulder.

"Tim. In all seriousness, I wanted to say congratulations regarding your relationship with..."—he then hesitated for just a beat, not sure what to call her before settling on the safest name—"the president. All of us who know you are truly happy for you. Just as all of us who know you have tremendous respect for the president."

Shannon looked over at Richards in real appreciation. As he did, his eyes teared up unexpectedly.

"Thank you for saying that, Bill," answered Shannon as he picked up the white linen napkin before him and quickly dabbed his eyes. "Sorry about the waterworks, here. Not sure where that came from."

"A good place," stressed Jensen. "The best place. Listen, Tim. I very strongly second what Bill just said. I've known Carolina for a long time. She is in fact one of my best friends in life and, quite possibly, the best person I have ever known. I have never seen her light up the way she has when she lets her guard down around you. As you know...as we *all* know...she's had a very tough life. On top of that, she ended up marrying a real shithead. Now she's a single mom and, oh, by the way, president of the United States during the most unreal and dangerous crisis the world has ever known."

"Yeah," interrupted Shannon. "Hence, my emotions just now. My timing with regard to her and our relationship could have been better."

"On the contrary," answered Jensen as he leaned closer. "It could *not* be better. If ever there was a time she needed a soul mate and someone to lean on emotionally, it's now."

Shannon was touched by the words and support from his two friends and seemed to be struggling for his next words.

Jensen sensed that now was the time to not only lighten the mood but get everyone refocused.

"Oh, and by the way," Jensen said with a smile. "Just because you're now the president's boyfriend, or First Man, or whatever title the media's going to give you, don't let that go to your head and start thinking you're going to take *my* job away from me."

Shannon knew what Jensen was doing and was deeply grateful for the humanity behind the words.

"Your job. *Your* job," laughed Shannon as he wiped his eyes one final time. "Screw that. I'm only in this so Carolina can name me the next commissioner of the NFL. *That's* where the real power and money is."

* * *

THREE MINUTES AFTER THE TWO COFFEES, one Coke, and plate of French fries were delivered to the table, the fries were gone. Not only did Jensen and Richards realize that they were indeed great comfort food, but they went really well with White House coffee.

Once the plate was taken away and the beverages replenished, Jensen asked that they not be disturbed unless he waved someone over.

"So," Jensen began as he looked at the two of them. "Now that the 'suits'—so to speak—are not here, what do you guys *really* think?"

Richards took a deep breath and let it out quickly. As if he was hoping for the question.

"With all due respect to the building I am now sitting in and the office it represents, I'd say we are sitting fucking ducks. *Sitting fucking ducks.* Not only did these assholes slime out of the pages of history and appear out of nowhere, but they kicked us in the balls to announce themselves. Worse than that, they can gouge our eyes out at literally any second, completely blind us, and then shove them up our ass at will."

"Please don't sugarcoat it, Bill," said Shannon with a purposeful smile. "I think we can handle the unvarnished truth."

With his question, Jensen had opened the steam valve on Richards, and a decade-plus of directed resentment was now spewing out.

Richards looked over at Shannon and shook his head.

"Please keep in mind that I don't consider the president one of them when I say this, but...screw these politicians. Screw *all* of them. Well over ninety percent of those bastards are gutless cowards who have long put their self-interests and the interests of their particular political party *well* before the needs of their constituents or the welfare of our nation. In a number of real ways, they helped to create and now *own* a great deal of this nightmare we now find ourselves in. As we are sitting here in this room, those friggin' Hitler Youth maggots on the moon can hit us again. They could vaporize DC while I'm sipping this coffee from this *fine* White House china. Why? Because those *jerks* in Congress and virtually every person who sat in the Oval Office went all Pollyanna on our asses and decided that our nation didn't need a military presence in space to protect our national security on Earth. Instead of seeing the world as it is, they took their marching orders from the scum that inhabits the United Nations and the latest generation of 'peaceniks' who preached it would be 'mean' and even 'un-American' to 'militarize' space. Well...*how* do you like us now? This is not about politics and it's not about ideology. I honestly can't stand either political party. We all want peace. My *very* job—along with the oath I swore—is about keeping the peace and protecting this nation from all enemies...foreign or domestic. Well, now we have a foreign...and *alien*...enemy on steroids. And from the edge of our atmosphere right down to the surface of the moon, we are basically defenseless."

"Well..." began Jensen as he turned to look over his shoulder. "We do have your toys."

"What? The X-39s?" asked Richards.

Jensen had personally approved the launching of the X-39. The vehicle was a manned version of the Air Force's highly secret X-37B program first launched in 2010. At its peak, the X-37B had stayed in orbit continuously for over eight hundred days while evaluating various military applications.

The X-39—overseen by the Air Force Rapid Capabilities Office—was a larger, sleeker, and deadly two-crewed next-generation model.

Since first being launched, the Air Force had continually kept one X-39 secretly in orbit around the Earth 24/7-365, with its two-man crews carrying out highly classified assignments.

"Yeah, them," answered Jensen.

Richards paused as he mentally went over schematics and actual capabilities.

"Close in, they can maybe do some damage. Maybe. I don't know. All I know is...I have a splitting headache at the moment."

Jensen was not surprised. Precisely because of the situation they were in, the secretary of defense knew that every emotion, be it the tears of Shannon or the rage now displayed by Richards, was right below the surface begging and needing to come out.

To a certain extent, Jensen knew that process was healthy and would serve to help clear troubled minds.

Jensen waved over the steward and asked for a packet of aspirin.

After it was delivered and then taken by Richards, Jensen held up his hands to both of them in a plea.

"Look, in one way or another, we are all military guys. This is the biggest SNAFU shit-storm of our lives. We *all* know the mistakes that got us into this mess. The fact is, we can't go back and fix a goddamn one. Not one. So…what I need…what *we* need…is *any* idea that will give us some breathing room to think, to strategize, and then to fight back. *If not…*"

Those last two words hung in the air like the blade of a guillotine about to scream down to cut through an exposed and unprotected neck.

# 37

After the diatribe by Lunar Hitler, Stewart and Washington were unchained and led down a staircase to the floor of the arena. There, each had a thick black plastic ring placed around their necks and then tightened. Each ring was attached to a ten-foot, thin metal pole.

The poles were now held by one of the super-monstrous beings from Lunar Hitler's security detail. Beings who nearly jerked Stewart and Washington completely off their feet as they dragged and guided them toward the audience of ten thousand now baying storm troopers.

There were three aisles separating the still standing storm troopers.

After being led twenty feet down the first aisle, which ran three hundred feet, Stewart knew the drill. By the time he was halfway down the five-foot-wide aisle, he was covered from head to toe in spit and mucus spat upon him by storm troopers who looked deranged enough to kill him at any second.

Aside from the spit and the mucus, Stewart was shoved, kicked, and had various objects from cups to boots thrown at his head.

With his eyes now burning from the spit and mucus, he tried to turn his head to locate Venus. When he did, he knew he was getting off easy compared to her.

Just as he saw her, one of the female storm troopers walked up to her, slapped her hard across the face, and then unsheathed an enormous combat knife that was encased on her right thigh. She took the knife and cut off most of Washington's space suit and her water-cooled nylon undergarments until she was all but naked.

When done, the female storm trooper gleefully took the pole from the male and proceeded to parade Washington along the rest of the aisle. As she did, now openly drooling male storm troopers darted into the aisle to grope any and all of Washington's body.

As Washington's piercing scream of terror and revulsion suddenly filled the arena, the massive being holding Stewart's pole got distracted for just a second as he tried to take in the sight for his own perverse pleasure. He then loosened his grip just enough for Stewart to break free and sprint toward one of the beings violating Washington.

Before the collected storm troopers realized what had happened, Stewart was able to cover the twenty feet in front of him, sweep the legs out from under the drooling molester, and stomp him hard twice in what Stewart hoped were his tiny, inadequate Nazi balls.

Just as the right heel of his space boot landed for the second time with enough force to elicit a scream of pain from the fallen and shocked storm trooper, Stewart's world went black and silent.

* * *

THE LIGHT WAS HURTING his eyes a bit, and Stewart wondered if he had fallen asleep again on the outdoor sofa on the patio of his small ranch-style home in the subdivision of Timber Cove in Seabrook, Texas.

As Seabrook was just about thirty miles southeast of Houston, and Stewart didn't feel it was proper for him to openly root for the Patriots anymore, he'd adopted the Texans as at least his unofficial new team.

Stewart had never been much of a drinker, but once in a while he would have a Sam Adams or two while watching the Texans in his family room and then go outside to stretch out on the sofa of his screened-in patio after the game.

On more than one occasion, the setting sun hit Stewart squarely in his eyes and had woken him up. Once it did, rather than get up and go inside, the still somewhat groggy astronaut would simply turn his body away from the offending sunlight and go back to sleep.

Which is exactly what he intended to do now.

Except…when he tried to turn from the light, he found that he could not move. At all.

He managed to turn his head slightly. At that point, he heard the voice.

"If you don't smarten up, American, they will kill you the next time for sure."

Stewart wanted to open his eyes to see who was talking to him. He wanted to, but they seemed so heavy and he was still so tired after having his two beers. Plus, it was most likely just voices in his head from the Sam Adams.

"Two beers. What a wimp you are," Stewart mumbled to himself with a little laugh.

"No beers, American," the mystery voice volunteered. "You've lost a lot of blood and have a concussion from getting kicked multiple times in the head. A head which now has forty stiches in it."

*The voice of a neighbor,* Stewart wondered. He knew all of his immediate neighbors, and none of them spoke English with a German accent.

He didn't want to open his eyes. He wanted to go back to sleep.

But now, he also wanted to solve the riddle of the mystery voice.

Female to be sure. And also young sounding. Maybe the mystery voice was pretty.

He secretly wanted it to be his neighbor from around the corner. She had gone to North Texas State, become a Dallas Cowboys Cheerleader, was first runner-up in the Miss Texas contest, and was considered—at least by his fellow astronauts living in Timber Cove—to be the most beautiful woman around.

But this was still weird.

Even if that was her, why would she be speaking to him with a *German* accent? Second, why would she be speaking to him *at all*, as she was married to a very successful hedge fund manager and was building a fourteen-thousand-square-foot home up in the Woodlands thirty miles north of Houston.

*No way it can be her,* concluded Stewart. *Still, it's a nice voice, so I'll just take a quick peek and then go right back to sleep.*

At that, Stewart forced his eyelids up at least a millimeter and saw a blurry image of a person in a white coat standing a few feet away from him holding a small flashlight. He then blinked several times in rapid succession to try and clear his eyes.

Though it worked at taking away most of the blurriness, he knew he either still wasn't quite seeing clearly or was possibly having a dream.

Had to be a dream.

For, next to him was a tall woman with a very athletic figure who was wearing some type of royal-blue jumpsuit covered by a white lab coat opened at the front.

She had long black hair pulled back in some kind of ponytail, extremely dark eyes, and just a hint of makeup and red lipstick touching up the most beautiful face Stewart had ever seen in his life.

Because she made the former runner-up to Miss Texas look like a troll in search of a bridge to live under, Stewart now was positive he was still trapped in a dream.

Knowing that, he closed his eyes in the hope the dream would continue and somehow improve.

"*American*," the German-accented voice now said in a louder and seemingly annoyed tone. "Wake up. I need your mind clear when I speak with you."

As Stewart tried to contemplate the sudden attitude, the voice now yelled at him.

"*American!*"

Stewart reluctantly reopened his eyes to find the most beautiful face he had ever seen now hovering just six inches above his.

"Wow," he began to slur out. "You are very tall, but not as tall as the monsters in the arena."

The woman stared down at him without expression.

"Our height and size is partly due to the fact that our gravity is one-sixth yours on Earth. That, and over sixty years ago, the Nazi scientists here found a way to dramatically manipulate our DNA. Make us much bigger. Stronger. Much more aggressive. At least… some of us," answered the woman as she stood up straight and grabbed the stethoscope around her neck.

Stewart was still coming in and out of it. Trying to focus on the voice and especially that face.

"And *who* are you? I like you. You are beautiful and haven't kicked my ass…yet."

The woman shook her head while offering an inkling of a smile.

"My name, American, is Irena Oberth. We are in a private clinic reserved only for the flag officers. I am your doctor. Or, at least, I will be until they finally execute you."

# 38

"Okay," said Tim Shannon. "In addition to going old school back to 1960s technology, as Bill said, we've got to do two things as fast as humanly possible. First, build a small fleet of those space fighters, and second, somehow take the fight to the Nazis before they come to us."

"Well," began Jensen again, now in a whisper. "With regard to your first ask, we actually have that."

Shannon wrinkled his forehead. "Have what?"

"The small fleet. We have one."

Shannon shook his head. "Are you talking the X-39 again? We only have two of those."

Jensen smiled like the cat who just ate the canary.

"Nope. We actually have twelve of them now."

"What the hell?!" proclaimed Shannon as his voice rose. "I'm only the head of NASA. How come I don't know about this?"

"Need to know and all that shit," answered Jensen as he motioned Shannon to lower his voice. "We don't have time for anyone to get

166

all high and mighty at the moment. The ten additional X-39s were part of an off-the-books black program. Too many members of Congress leak to too many members of the media, so we kept the circle very small on that one."

"You've got that right," said Richards.

"Wait a minute," said Shannon as he sat back in his chair. "You knew about this?"

"Yeah," Richards said with a smile as he rubbed his temples. "Of course. My guys have to fly them."

Shannon's mind was now racing.

"Wait a minute. Does the president know about these 'off the books' black program spacecraft?"

Jensen showed the good grace to pretend he was somewhat shamed by the question.

"Ah, no. The need to tell her hadn't quite come up yet."

Shannon held out his arms.

"Do you think fuckin' Nazis on the moon nuking us means it's time to tell her?"

"Good point," answered Jensen as he stroked his beard while imagining how *that* conversation would soon play out.

* * *

"Okay," jumped in Richards to get them back on track. "Let's all assume that we have some time here. We don't have any other choice, really. We build, we push, we fight, until all of this is either a deep, black smoking crater where Washington, DC used to be or until we figure out a way to stand up to them. As the boxer Mike Tyson said way back in the late '80s, 'Everyone's got a plan until they get punched in the face.' These Nazis may not expect to get hit back. And once they do, maybe they'll make a mistake that gives us any kind of opening. Maybe the X-39 can give us that opening."

"Shit, Bill," moaned Jensen as he ran his right hand over his smooth scalp. "X-39 or not, we don't even know who '*they*' are. Almost every single word coming out of our mouths is based on an assumption or guess. Is it ten people? One hundred? A thousand? What?"

"You're right," added Shannon, who was forcing himself to calm down after being told he was out of the loop. "We don't know. But the look of that vehicle in the photo that my communications person found doesn't say 'we're a band of crazy Nazis hiding on the moon and playing war games.' It says to me that it looked like a very impressive vehicle. Better than anything we've sent to the moon in the past, and better than anything we have on the drawing board now. It says to me to remember what the foundation of the Nazi Party accomplished in secret from the end of World War I until the beginning of World War II. It says to me that there's something very professional, very proficient, and *very* planned about whoever is up there. The nuclear bombs they built scream that *louder* than anything. And remember, they chose now to come out of hiding and hit us. They picked the timing."

"I still don't know if I totally agree with that," said Richards as he shook his head. "I still believe there's at least an even chance that we forced their hand somehow. Did they have a plan? I believe for sure. They didn't build those nukes to use as coffee tables. They built them with the intent to use them against Earth. But maybe not quite yet. Whatever the truth, in some ways, this is all about to become the now politically incorrect phrase of 'cowboys versus Indians' again. Or, much more accurately *and* politically correct, vastly outgunned Native American warriors against the entire United States calvary and government."

"Well," said Jensen. "Sparing us the 'collective guilt of our nation' lesson, what's your point?"

"My point," answered Richards as he sat back in his chair, "is that, pound for pound, the best fighters our nation ever had were the Native American warriors. I should correct myself and say they were the best fighters this *land* has ever known before it became *our nation* due to some truly disgusting and backstabbing circumstances employed against various Native American tribes. Can't get around that 'shared collective guilt,' I'm afraid. But no matter that sordid chapter of our past, I believe we *will* soon be *them* and need to channel that kind of knowledge, skill, courage, and sacrifice. We need to learn to become invisible to this enemy, hit them when they least expect it and are most vulnerable, and then maneuver to hit them again and again. Many times, over many battles, those outgunned Native American tribes and warriors won because of stealth, intimidation, attrition, and, quite frankly, the vicious and unyielding determination of someone defending their homeland and families against merciless invaders. Last time I checked, the Nazis were the personification of 'merciless invaders.'"

Jensen shook his head.

"I don't know about the Native American analogy. I think the Polish, French, and Dutch resistance movements in World War II work much better here, but your basic point is well taken. We have to morph into the badass resistance now. And what I especially agree with is that we need some more expertise at this table and advising POTUS right away..."

"POTUS?" asked Richards as he wrinkled his forehead.

"Sorry," Jensen replied. "I forgot you come to us from outside the toxic DC bubble. 'POTUS' is the acronym and shorthand we use for 'president of the United States.' Now, in my opinion, we need to get the very best experts on Nazi and World War II history here immediately. And next, we need to speak with the chancellors of Germany and Austria to give them all the intelligence we have to date. This unbelievable news that we have to share is going to hit them very hard, but they still may know something we don't. Something that may help. But first…I have to fess up and tell the president about our little fleet of X-39s."

# 39

A quarter of a mile away from the infirmary where Stewart was being held, Reichsführer Manfred Beck, the commander in chief of both the Lunar SS and Lunar Luftwaffe, was about to hold court behind the closed doors of a heavily guarded conference room.

He was in a foul mood, and those at the conference table before him knew it. Even before they had entered the meeting, they had heard that he had personally shot one of his own men for killing one of the American invaders.

Joining Reichsführer Beck at the meeting was Alfred Hadler, the head of the Lunar Gestapo, Ludwig von Fritsch, the field marshal of the Lunar Army, and Helene Willhaus, the Reichsminister for Information.

"Where is the Führer?" asked Willhaus with a twisted smile.

Both Hadler and von Fritsch resented her being in the room, but for the last two years, she had been Beck's partner and had quickly, cleverly, and ruthlessly parlayed their physical relationship into a powerful and feared position.

Feared, because on occasion, it was known that she would whisper into the ear of Beck regarding someone she disliked and falsely accuse them of plotting against the Fatherland. Soon thereafter, that person would disappear down a bottomless lunar crevasse.

"He put in his needed performance," said the Reichsführer with an edge to his voice. "It is still best that we not discuss his role—even in private—until the ultimate completion of our mission."

"This is a very dangerous game you are playing, Manfred," said von Fritsch.

Beck instantly shot the field marshal a dark and warning look.

"My apologies," added von Fritsch as he offered a mock bow from his seated position, "*Reichsführer.*"

Alfred Hadler also stared hard at the field marshal. While he understood the point von Fritsch was getting at, ultimately, it did not matter.

Since childhood, he had sworn his entire allegiance to Beck. His life was dedicated to the protection and advancement of the greatest leader this new world of theirs had ever known in its short history.

A leader who was not only capable of avenging the crimes committed against them by the dogs of Earth but returning the Fatherland to its rightful place of power over their previous world, as well as the current one.

Without moving his head, the chief of the Gestapo shifted his ice-blue eyes to take in Helene Willhaus. Hadler considered her nothing more than an opportunist. But a very dangerous one.

He knew her to be intelligent, merciless, and single-mindedly ambitious.

To her detriment, he also knew those traits made her reckless and ultimately…a risk.

He fully intended to move against her, but first he had to wait for Beck to grow tired of her company. An eventuality that may have been greatly accelerated by her latest ill-conceived move.

As much as Hadler hated the Americans, he agreed with von Fritsch that parading and humiliating the female American astronaut before the soldiers was a mistake.

*She,* thought Hadler as his penetrating gaze never left Willhaus, *had talked the Reichsführer into it. She convinced him that it would galvanize the troops to see the insult of the Americans sending a minority woman to their sacred home on the moon.*

Fortunately, von Fritsch was able to intercede and remind the Reichsführer of the role this American woman would have to play later, and was able to have him stop the group assault.

Six of von Fritsch's elite Waffen-SS soldiers had then whisked her away to a holding cell, where she was heavily sedated and put under protective custody to ensure she did not try to take her own life.

Hadler knew that incident had contributed to the Reichsführer's steadily darkening mood. He had been talked into something against his better judgment, and he resented it.

*Good,* thought Hadler. *Resent it. You have but one mission. Don't let that witch impair your thinking. The Earth-born half-breeds are finally upon us. Let us stick to your glorious plan to exterminate them and take back what is rightfully ours.*

No sooner did Hadler complete the thought than Beck's colossal right fist slammed down on and dented the metallic conference table.

"Stupid!" he screamed to the room.

"Stupid," he emphasized again as he turned his gaze upon Willhaus. "We can afford *zero* mistakes as we prepare to fully launch this operation, and I just approved one against my own instincts. I am at fault. *Me.* I allowed my mind to be clouded by emotion. I will *never* make that same error again."

Even when Beck's fist crashed down on the table, Hadler never took his eyes off of Willhaus. As Beck's words of controlled rage spilled out in her direction, she shifted her own eyes to look at Hadler for a millisecond, only to find him staring at her with unblinking and undisguised revulsion.

"I need," continued Beck as he lowered the volume of his words but not their intended displeasure. "*We* need...these two Americans to not only remain alive but functional. Field Marshal von Fritsch was right to approach me when he did. What if, as he asked, the American woman chose to kill herself or permanently harmed herself in the attempt? And then...and then...the male American astronaut broke free and did what I would have done in just such a situation. And because he did...because we put on that needless and juvenile spectacle...he was almost fatally injured by several soldiers and is now in the infirmary."

Beck stopped to ball up both of his hands that were gripping the edge of the conference table.

"Stupid!" he screamed out again. "We could have lost both of them and may well still lose their usefulness to us. And for what? *For what?* A mindless prank to humiliate the female American in an act which may still only punish *us.*"

He then stood up with such force that his chair flew against the wall behind him and bounced several times before clattering into a corner.

"Enough!" Beck yelled. "No more errors. No more mistakes in judgment. *No more.* The time is upon us. We have prepared for this moment since that vermin first landed upon our world in 1969. We are ready. Nobody can stop us but...us. And *that,*" he emphasized as he looked first at Willhaus before settling on Hadler with an all but imperceptible nod, "will never be allowed to happen. *Never.*"

Beck turned and took three steps and grabbed the handle of the door. As he did, he turned one last time to look at the three of them.

"I am going down to the infirmary to check on the condition of the male American. When I come back, I want all of my generals prepared to meet with me."

As the Reichsführer flew out the door, Helene Willhaus instantly tried to ascertain the true meaning of the look shared by Beck and Hadler.

When she quickly looked over at Hadler only to discover he had never taken his eyes off of her, she had her answer.

# 40

"Gentlemen," said the president's personal assistant as he walked up to the three men at the table at the back of the White House Mess. "The president has asked that you join her in the Situation Room right away."

\* \* \*

ONCE ALL WERE RECONVENED, the president got right back to business.

"Presidents Li and Medvedev have not only agreed to meet with me here in Washington, but they will round up those under their respective spheres of influence who they feel can definitely contribute to the cause. We will naturally do the same, and then we will have what will amount to a 'joint session of the world' in the chamber for the House of Representatives at the Capitol."

"When?" asked Jensen on behalf of those who were not privy to the teleconference.

"Since 'right this minute' could still be too late, I have instructed the vice president to utilize his staff and get everything ready as fast as humanly possible. He is off doing that now while also reaching out to our allies to inform them of the upcoming meeting. We will meet as soon as possible with as many as can show up."

The president then turned back to look at Richards.

"Colonel, if you could finish up your elevator pitch as fast as possible, I will then leave it to you, Secretary Jensen, General McNamara, the administrator of NASA, and all others in your relevant chains of command to come up with the best strategy for not only our defense, but ultimately, our complete victory."

"Yes, Madam President," answered Richards as he stole a quick look at Jensen, McNamara, and Shannon. "The most basic elements of the paper I wrote back then hypothesizing about fighting an enemy based upon the moon are these: In conjuncture with Russia, China, India, Japan, the United Kingdom, France, Canada, Israel, and the various private space contractors in our nation and around the world, we must get every piece of off-the-shelf space technology ready for the fight. Every piece…"

Shannon picked that time to clear his throat and look across the table at Jensen.

"Mike. On that subject, isn't there something you would like to tell the president?"

Carolina Garcia knew Shannon well enough by now to detect the hint of anger in his voice.

She looked over at her secretary of defense.

"Mike?" she asked as she looked quickly at Tim before coming back to the man who was just put on the spot.

"Yes, Madam President," answered Jensen as all at the table noted that he had not used her first name this time. "We can get into all of this in more depth if you like, but with regard to the X-39 currently in orbit, and the other attached to a Titan III C out at Vandenberg, I'm…uh…happy to report that we have ten more built and ready to go."

Jensen—and the rest of the room—waited for the president to explode with the realization that she had been kept in the dark with regard to such a critically important asset. Instead, she simply sat silent and stared at Jensen for a solid ten count.

He would have preferred she screamed at him.

"Okay," she finally answered with a bit of a condescending smile. "I will take that as good news. Ten more of our secret space fighters kept *secret* from me…now at our immediate disposal. Excellent. But…still on the ground, you say?"

"Yes, Madam President," answered the SecDef.

"Well," began the president as she looked quickly at everyone in the room. "I am not a historian, but if memory serves, when the Japanese attacked Pearl Harbor on December 7th, 1941, they destroyed a great many of our aircraft…on the ground."

"Yes, ma'am," Jensen replied as his face began to blush in response to the nonconfrontational ass kicking the president was giving him. It would leave no marks but hurt twice as much.

"So," she said with her little smile still firmly in place. "If you, Colonel Richards, and Tim agree, maybe it would be best to get them fully stocked, fully fueled, fully armed, and launched as soon as possible."

In spite of himself, Tim Shannon smiled in pure pride at the command displayed by the love of his life. At the same instant, he looked over at Jensen and nodded to convey that they were good.

Jensen immediately winked back and then turned to the president.

"Yes, Carolina," answered Jensen. "I'll give that order as soon as we conclude this meeting."

"Excellent," stated Garcia as she rubbed her hands together. "With that bit of good news now deposited in our positivity bank, perhaps Colonel Richards can continue with…and conclude…his briefing."

"Yes, Madam President," answered Richards, who suddenly felt like he was once again in over his head.

"So…aside from getting every bit of our off-the-shelf rockets and technology ready, we must begin immediate construction of mini-communications systems and micro-satellites. Hundreds of them. All built in a hardened facility and all meant to be disposable. If the Nazis destroy one, we send up ten more to take its place. Next, and I should stress that this is all in no particular order at the moment, we will need to take the fight *to* the enemy…"

"The Nazis," punctuated the president.

"Yes, ma'am," Richards acknowledged. "Sorry. We need to take the fight to the *Nazis* on the moon as soon as we can…*if* we can. When that time comes, we would *not* engage them right away. Rather, we would make them dizzy with landings. Confuse them. Divert whatever military assets they may have up there. Announce to the world—on a channel or channels we can be sure they would be monitoring—that we are sending a manned military force to the moon in those spacecraft. Most would be empty and unmanned. Again, dummy landings to divert their forces and attention. We have the technology to simulate conversations from within those empty-shell landers to make the Nazis believe they are manned. Then, as we drop these various landers around the surface of the moon, we sprinkle in the real deal. Elite commandos already in training by the Space Corps—along with those from other nations—to take up strategic positions on the moon. By that point the Nazis will either assume it's another dummy landing or ignore it to conserve their strength. Again, assuming the worst means assuming they have a significant military presence on the moon. But even at that, the moon is a very large body. Very large. About one-fourth the size of Earth or equivalent in square miles to the continent of Asia. Again, meaning relatively speaking, it's a very big place and potentially easy to hide several strike teams on or within its surface. Also, Madam President, it should be noted that militarily, it's much harder to take out a target on the moon. Because there is no atmosphere, there are no blast effects and no pressure waves from whatever weapon we might detonate near the target. Also, because the target is already on the moon means it's built to withstand thermal spikes of a very high order. Now, if we use nukes, then the radiation from that could be effective, but again, only if you hit the target on the nose..."

"Colonel," interrupted the president. "I don't want to get too deep into the weeds here. You've just outlined random parts of a plan based upon a great many assumptions. Bottom line, tell me what *worries* you about all of this."

Richards paused as he closed his eyes for a second and ran both of his hands across his face as if cleaning a slate.

"What worries me...is that they *know* all of this. *They* know it. That they have been up there for over eighty years and know the moon like the back of their own hands. It is part of their very being. Because of that, their military leaders and scientists would know that, eventually—no matter how difficult the task—we would figure out a way to hit them, and their lunar base, lunar colony, or even lunar cities would be subject to partial or complete destruction. Those bases, colonies, or cities representing the *entirety* of their population and species. So...they would want to make sure we could *never* take the fight to them. Ever."

"How would the Nazis ensure that, Colonel?"

"Again, Madam President, it would have to be a combination of them basically taking out all of our—and by 'our,' I mean the world's—communications and military satellites while simultaneously launching a space force large enough to not only guarantee complete military dominion of the space between the atmosphere of the Earth and the moon, but to protect whatever doomsday weapon they would launch along with that fleet."

Some of the blood actually drained out of the president's face.

"*Doomsday weapon*," she more whispered to herself than anyone in the room.

"Yes, Madam President," answered Richards, ignoring the rhetorical intent of her comment. "*The* worst-case scenario. A new master plan from the new 'master race.'"

The president shook her head once and then stood.

"Well, Colonel. Let's hope and pray that your worst-case scenario is wrong. At the same time, we must assume it is correct. Therefore...*save us*. That's all you and everyone gathered at this table have to do. Not too much pressure. Get to work."

# 41

With his own four-man security detail in tow, Reichsführer Beck burst through the doors of the infirmary to find Dr. Oberth taking the blood pressure of the male American astronaut.

He stopped three feet from them and swiveled his head back and forth before looking down upon the five-foot, eleven-inch doctor.

"Where is your nurse?" asked Beck in a sharp tone, referring to the young woman who had come up through the ranks of the Lunar Hitler Youth and was trained to keep an eye on the doctors in this facility and then report back regularly to the Gestapo.

"I sent her to get supplies," answered Oberth. "She should be back momentarily."

The eight-foot, four-inch behemoth of Beck leaned down to stare intently at the face and closed eyes of Stewart. He then flicked his eyes to look at the swelling and bandage on the right side of Stewart's head.

"Has he regained consciousness yet?"

"No, Herr Reichsführer. Not as of yet."

"Will he live?"

"Yes, Herr Reichsführer. His vitals are getting stronger with each minute. But he suffered a severe concussion. His mind may come out of it in ten minutes, ten hours, or ten days. That is not up to me."

Beck stepped closer until she could feel his hot breath falling upon her head and smell its foul odor.

"Remember, mongrel. We let you and the other hideous imperfections to our race like you live so that you may serve us. You are allowed zero failures. *Zero*. Your life—and let me remind you, the lives of your next-to-useless academic parents—depends upon you doing your job to perfection. To perfection and to the letter of *my* orders. If he dies, you and your parents die. Pray that he wakes up...soon."

With that, Beck did an about-face and stormed out of the room toward his next meeting.

\* \* \*

"AMERICAN," WHISPERED OBERTH. "You can open your eyes now. *American*. Now. We don't have much time."

Stewart opened his eyes to find the doctor staring nervously at the door. Just before Beck had almost taken its hinges off with his entrance, Oberth had instructed Stewart to pretend to still be unconscious no matter who entered the room.

Oberth turned back to look down at Stewart.

"There you have it," whispered the doctor. "That monster explained it much more quickly and clearer than I ever could have to convince you. Like you, they consider me and those like me here on the moon to be nothing more than half-breeds. We don't look like them. We didn't grow to be as tall and strong as them. And we don't think in maniacal, revenge-centric lockstep like them. We actually choose to think for ourselves. My—"

There was a noise out in the hallway, and Oberth turned in terror to look back at the door. After twenty seconds of staring at the still closed door, she let out the breath she had been holding and turned back to Stewart.

"My great-grandfather," continued Oberth in now the lowest of whispers possible, "is the one who designed and built the rockets which first got him and the other survivors to the moon in 1945. My great-grandfather was a genius. Really just a boy genius who dreamed of getting himself and others into space. He was not a soldier. He was not a Nazi. He was a simple, single-minded rocket scientist who only wanted to conquer the academic challenge of getting humans to space and then the moon. He got us here. But at a very steep price. The Gestapo took his wife and small son hostage to ensure his complete cooperation. Then, twelve years after they landed here and it was clear they were on the way to self-sufficiency, the representatives of that same Gestapo sent to the moon labeled him a 'threat to the Fatherland,' chained him to a stake in one of the outer airlocks without a space suit, and then opened that airlock to the vacuum of the moon and space. He died in the most cruel and grotesque of ways. An execution they not only filmed but play at least once a year on our viewing devices as a reminder of the punishment that awaits those they accuse of being traitors."

"I'm sorry," Stewart started to say in a raspy voice at normal volume. "But, why—"

Oberth did two things in rapid succession.

The first was to clamp her right hand over Stewart's mouth to stop him from talking further. Then, when it was clear he got the message via the hand on his mouth and the fear conveyed in her dark eyes, she let go, walked two steps to a table next to his bed, picked up a metallic bottle full of water with a bent-metal straw, and brought the straw over to Stewart's lips.

Stewart took several long sips of the proffered water and then nodded when done.

"Sorry," he himself now whispered. "Sorry first for speaking too loud. And second, I'm still sorry that I don't understand why you are telling me all of this."

"Why?" asked the young doctor as she leaned closer down to Stewart in clear frustration. "*Why?* Because you are a once in a life-time opportunity, and I may only have seconds left to speak with you. Maybe because for the first time in my life on this macabre imitation of a civilization, I see the faintest light of hope. Earth is *that* hope. I am not alone, American. That monster just mentioned my parents. I am here to tell you that there are hundreds of us who hate these Nazis. *Hundreds.* We hate these fiends who have punished, imprisoned, or executed our families and friends. Like every dictatorial regime back on your Earth, those who rule here with an iron fist are petrified of intellectual thought, reason, common sense, and most especially any and all questioning of their megalomaniac ambitions. So *why* am I telling you all of this? Because it's you or nothing, American. You or *nothing.* You need to know what you are up against. What—"

"Wait," pleaded Stewart. "*Please,* wait a second. I can't think. I can't process. My head is pounding, and it sounds like your voice is coming through cotton balls. I just…I mean…this has all been a whirlwind of surreal impossibilities. One after another. Nazis on the moon. My friend murdered by a storm trooper. Adolf Hitler—I still can't believe the name *Hitler* is coming out of my mouth—somehow alive and in his prime. And now you. Unloading—pardon me— this crap on me. Why? To save yourself? To lure me into some trap created by that fucking freak who just walked out of here? Why?"

"You are *so* stupid, American," hissed Oberth as she jabbed her right index finger into Stewart's chest. "I can't believe your country picked such a *dummkopf* to lead their first mission here since 1972. America must be a nation full of moronic sheep if they hold you out as one of their best..."

Stewart couldn't help himself and smiled with the insults while simultaneously saying "Ouch."

"Don't smile at me, you stupid, stupid man. Just the fact that you smile confirms my opinion of your lack of intelligence while also telling me that you have no idea what you are up against. Just me talking to you not only puts my life in grave danger, but more importantly to me, the lives of my parents and many others."

"So again, why even take such a risk by telling me all this stuff?" asked Stewart after ditching the smile.

Oberth turned to look back at the door again before leaning down to face Stewart. "Because, as I just *told* you, it's you or nothing. Your planet Earth is facing complete annihilation and—"

"Complete annihilation?" said Stewart as he shook his head back and forth. "Wait. You can't be serious. I know those storm troopers are huge and evil, but there are only thousands of them. Even if they could somehow get down to the surface of Earth, what can they do against a worldwide collective standing army of over seventy million plus thousands of nuclear warheads?"

"You fool," she said in almost resigned anger. "I am twenty-seven years old and since I was a child, I have watched selected broadcasts from your world which were approved by our censors. One of the expressions which always rang most true to me is, '*Those who forget history are doomed to repeat it.*'"

"I don't need a history lesson, *Fraulein*."

Oberth now laughed down at him.

"I don't have the time to give you all the lessons you need, you stupid American. So just *one* for now. Clearly, that's all your tiny little brain can handle at the moment."

Stewart actually chuckled at the latest insult and opened his eyes wider to take in the whole of the person, literally and figuratively, talking down to him.

"You and everyone else forget the history of Germany from just after World War I and the signing of the Treaty of Versailles to just before 1934. Hitler and the henchmen who licked his boots were born out of the injustice of that so-called treaty. The world thought they had neutered and humiliated Germany, but all they did was anger and inspire the leaders *and* the people—most of them good people at the time—to, in total secrecy, build the most powerful war machine the world had ever known. In the fifteen years after the signing of that treaty, Germany had an army of over one million soldiers, over one hundred warships, and over eight thousand aircraft. *Fifteen years*, American. An army and weapons that became the Nazi war machine. The point being that the monsters here who now rule the moon are super beings compared to the ones who accomplished that before World War II. *Super beings*. After almost a century on the moon, they have assembled hundreds of scientists. On Earth, those Nazis built the world's most feared war machine in *fifteen years*. *Imagine* what these super beings can do in *eighty years*. Especially when a majority of those scientists were tasked with but one assignment: to build the most powerful weapons ever. *Ever*, you stupid American. And two of them, I am very sad to report, have succeeded. They have succeeded. Surely, you have heard of directed-energy weapons. Well, I can say with complete confidence that these Nazi scientists have created the most powerful directed-energy weapon of all. Something that harnesses the light of the sun and magnifies it up to one million times its power and then concentrates that beam into—"

Just then, the door to the infirmary opened and a six-foot, five-inch blonde woman in a white nurse's uniform walked in carrying a plastic box full of medical supplies. She stopped five feet into the room and stared at Oberth and then the patient, who still seemed to be out cold.

"Doctor," she said as her eyes narrowed. "Did I hear you speaking to someone just before I walked into the room?"

Oberth quickly turned on her heel and walked over to the much taller and much more powerful woman. She smiled as she reached out and took the box of supplies from the nurse.

"Not talking, Helga. Singing. Simply singing one of the songs we were all taught as children which rightfully glorify our Fatherland while waiting for this disgusting American to awaken."

With her hands now free, the nurse slipped them into the front pockets of the white slacks she was wearing. There, her right hand wrapped around a small pistol the Lunar Gestapo had given her and which she had become an expert at using.

A weapon she longed to fire against *any* traitor to the Fatherland.

# 42

Reichsführer Beck walked into the largest conference room in the military wing of the Lunar Wolf Lair to find his top thirty generals and military officers already seated around the table.

Beck surveyed the room as was his want and then slowly took his place at the head of the table.

The seat to his right was filled by Field Marshal von Fritsch. The chair to his left was empty but soon to be taken by the man who walked into the room in his usual measured fashion.

Three seconds after entering the conference room, Alfred Hadler, the bespectacled, seven-foot-tall, precisely black-suited figure with the close-cropped gray hair, walked over to Beck, leaned down, and then whispered in the Reichsführer's left ear.

As Hadler then moved away and took his seat, Beck nodded his head once with just the hint of a smile appearing on his face. If one did not know better, the smile could have easily been mistaken for a facial tic.

On each side of the large conference table running along the wall were twenty chairs. As Beck looked to his left, those chairs were empty. To his right, ten of the chairs were filled by the Fatherland's top military scientist and his nine civilian subordinates.

It was the qualifications and current work assignment of the nine civilian scientists that most interested Beck at the moment. As he studied them one by one, three looked over toward him and then instantly began to stare at their feet as their heartbeats accelerated and their blood pressure rose.

Reichsführer Beck's gaze then settled upon the last two scientists in the row. The two who, not by coincidence as he knew, were seated farthest away from him. He looked at them intently until he was sure the weight of his stare caused the man and the woman to shift uncomfortably in their seats.

With that small and knowingly petty victory achieved, Beck turned his head to take in all gathered.

"Before we begin," started Beck as that slight muscle tic seemed to affect his lips again for a split second, "I want to send the greetings and gratitude of our Führer. As he is off meticulously planning this campaign, he has asked that I continue to lead these meetings in his stead and institute *his* orders. As we know him to be a conduit to God, serving him remains my—and *our*—highest honor. Next, it is my very sad duty to report that Reichsminister Willhaus is dead. Gruppenführer Hadler just informed me that Helene committed suicide a short time ago. I can most certainly confirm that the poor woman had a very troubled mind, and I fear that the growing responsibilities she was undertaking to help ensure our Fatherland's most glorious and just achievement was too much for her. Please…let us all bow our heads in a moment of silence for this tragic and most untimely passing."

All obediently bowed their heads, with the exception of Beck and Hadler.

With his right hand resting on the top of the table, Beck pointed his index finger at the male and female scientists sitting at the very end of the row along the wall and then looked over at Hadler.

Hadler compressed his thin lips together while nodding his head just once, as if confirming the subject of a previous conversation.

"So," said Beck loudly as he clapped his massive hands together and startled everyone back to his immediate attention. "Let's now get right to the *only* purpose of our meeting today. That being the Führer's plan for the complete destruction of every government and military on Earth and the planned enslavement of its entire population. When I am done, we will have a forced labor camp at our disposal that will number in the *billions*. And from that labor camp, we will select the eventual hundreds of thousands of infants we will indoctrinate and then use to expand our glorious Fatherland. Not only here on the moon…but deep into the solar system."

With Beck's last declaration, the female scientist at the end of the row let out an involuntary slight whimper. One the Reichsführer picked up.

"Ah, Frau Oberth. I had intended to address you and your husband later. But now is as good a time as any. Thank you for reminding me."

The husband and wife in their late forties exchanged a quick look of trepidation before staring down once again at their respective feet.

"I wanted to take a moment to personally congratulate you on the critically important work your daughter Irena—I believe your *only* child—is doing on behalf of the Fatherland. As we speak, she is attending to the medical needs of the American male swine astronaut who dared to assault one of my soldiers. You both must be so very proud to have such an accomplished young doctor as your daughter. So very proud…"

At that exact second, Beck slammed his fist once again onto the surface of the conference table. As most in the room jumped with the violence of the gesture, he stared with unadulterated hate in his eyes at the married scientists he was now addressing.

"Look at me when I speak to you," he screamed. "Surely, you would have taught your impressive daughter that basic manner and more."

As if flipping a switch, Beck then lowered his tone to that of polite conversation.

"Now, as Gruppenführer Hadler and others may have communicated to you in the past, because your daughter is so impressive and because she is doing such critically important work for us right now, I want to assure you that she will be under our *constant* observation and protection. This is, after all, the most exciting but possibly most stressful time in our brief history on our new world. As we just found out with regard to the late Reischminister Willhaus, stress, no matter how glorious the cause, can sometimes cause people to do strange and unexplained things. With that in mind, I promise you that we will keep the closest of eyes on your only child so that no harm befalls her."

As the Oberths reached for each other's hand and as their eyes filled with tears, Beck shifted his demonic gaze to take in the other seven civilian scientists in the row.

"Just as I can assure all of you," he announced in a growingly louder voice, "that Gruppenführer Hadler's Gestapo is watching and monitoring each of your children and *all* of your relatives to make doubly sure that no harm comes to them while you carry out the most important assignment in the history of our new Fatherland."

Beck paused to nod at his aide-de-camp and one of his two personal assistants. The young officer instantly poured a cup of steaming black coffee from the setup in the corner of the room and placed it before the Reichsführer.

As Beck watched the white wafts of steam rise from the cup, he allowed himself a small chuckle. *The Earthlings have no idea what they are up against,* he thought with great satisfaction.

None.

Eighty-four years ago, those who came before him to the moon brought every seed and every bean needed. Hundreds of pounds packed away in those primitive rockets.

The agronomists who came in those rockets quickly learned how to modify and then light the lunar soil they tilled below the surface of the moon. Over eight decades later, the massive nurseries hidden beneath their new world would rival or better any on Earth.

They had proudly carved out a completely self-sustaining home for themselves in but several decades. The discovery of water and helium-3 proved to be everything.

Everything.

Shelter, food, weapons, energy, transportation, and luxury. They had it all. They *built* and *reinvented* it all. No one had given them a thing. No one.

But, thought Beck to himself as he took a sip from his steaming cup of excellent German coffee, it was not enough. It was not *nearly* enough.

# 43

As the hot coffee passed over his lips, he thought of the Earthly expression: revenge is a dish best served cold.

*But…not in our case. In our case and as doled out by us, revenge is a dish best served hotter than the very fires of Hell.*

With that pleasure-giving image now planted in his mind, he turned toward his top military scientist.

"Otto. Is Operation Prometheus ready to launch?"

The weasel-looking human in Nazi garb smiled as he first looked toward the two scientists at the end of the row and then back over at Beck.

"Yes, my Reichsführer." He answered with a partial bow. "Thanks to the excellent work of the Oberths, we have succeeded in not only harnessing the power of the sun but turning it into the most powerful and lethal killing machine ever known to humanity."

Once again, Marie Oberth let out a small cry of anguish. At that same moment, her husband spoke out.

"That was never our intention. *Never*. We were trying to create a solar power satellite to power industry here on the moon. Unlimited and essentially free energy from the sun…forever."

Beck swiveled his chair just a fraction to look over at one of the members of his security detail. He then simply pointed toward the protesting scientist and waited.

The over eight-foot professional killer covered the ground between himself and Herr Oberth in three steps. He picked up the shocked scientist by the neck and backhanded him across the face.

Just once.

Once was enough to knock out two teeth and render the scientist unconscious.

Still holding the scientist suspended three feet off the floor, the storm trooper looked toward the Reichsführer.

Beck nodded once and the soldier dropped Oberth to the floor, where he folded upon himself like a limp washcloth.

Oberth's wife screamed and the storm trooper instantly lunged for her and lifted her off the floor before turning to look at Beck for instruction.

As the woman had gone quiet in terror, Beck motioned for the soldier to drop her.

"I need *silence* to think, Frau Oberth. You and your husband are disturbing my concentration so are no longer needed at this meeting. When your husband finally awakes, first please remind him *never* to address me unless I direct him to do so. And second, my sincere and unending thanks to him…and you…for your remarkable gift to the Fatherland. Why, after we incinerate a few million people on Earth *only* thanks to you and your collective genius, we might even erect a statue to the both of you in perpetual gratitude."

Beck looked down at the fallen figure of the scientist on the floor and then back up at the storm trooper who was still clutching the wife by the nape of her neck.

"Please escort the Oberths back to their quarters," ordered Beck with a satisfied smile.

After the couple was dragged and carried out of the room, Beck turned his attention to Hans Betz, the general under him who saw to the day-to-day needs of the Lunar Luftwaffe.

"General Betz. Is all in order and ready? We gave the dogs of Earth their wake-up call. Now, we must put them to sleep with Otto's new toy."

The general stood up at his seat at the conference table, picked up a remote control in front of him, pushed a button, and an eighty-inch flat screen television lowered from the ceiling.

"Yes, my Reichsführer. What you are about to see on the screen are our three Battle Stars. Because they will look like extremely bright stars in the nighttime sky to the people of Earth, we felt "Battle Star" was a most appropriate name. Each Battle Star will carry one Prometheus solar-powered satellite protected by fifteen space fighters and a crew of thirty. The space fighters, along with the Battle Star itself, are equipped with both directed-energy weapons as well as more conventional weapons. These weapons will be used, first, to destroy all of the satellites making modern life possible on Earth, and second, to defend against any missile launches or defensive attacks from Earth."

As the images of the Battle Stars popped up on the screen, Beck shot General Betz a worried look.

"Are our Battle Stars and Prometheus satellites vulnerable to attack from Earth?"

The general afforded himself a knowing laugh.

"No, my Reichsführer. No more than an eagle would worry about being hit with a pebble thrown by a diseased and dying rat. Each Battle Star and Prometheus satellite will be parked in a geosynchronous orbit about 22,300 miles above the Earth. One of the very first targets for our Prometheus satellites to incinerate will be the missile and rocket bases that might threaten us. Should the Earthlings manage to launch a missile before we have finished laying waste to those sites, our space fighters have plenty of time to intercept and destroy the missiles."

Beck seemed satisfied with the answer but far from at peace.

"Explain to me again—quickly—how our Prometheus weapons work."

"Yes, my Reichsführer," answered Betz while continuing to stand. "The beauty in all of this is that the Earthlings have done so much of the research for us. We simply improved upon it, then perfected it, and then in this particular case, transformed the research we intercepted into the ultimate instrument of *their* own destruction. That Russian troll of a writer Asimov wrote something about it in the early 1940s. Some Americans tried to make it a reality in the late 1970s. And then the Chinese put their own such solar power weapon into space just two years ago. A weapon one of our space fighters flew out to intercept and rendered useless soon after it was placed into Earth orbit. Now—"

"I don't need to know about the research, the history, or the science. I simply need to know the basics of how it will *work*, Hans," stressed Beck in growing impatience.

As Beck's lead general for the Lunar Luftwaffe, Betz was well used to his leader's mood swings and knew how to adapt accordingly.

"Of course, my Reichsführer. In a very real way, our Prometheus weapon is very much like the stories my grandfather told me of when he was a small boy back in our Fatherland on Earth. He would take a magnifying glass outside, find an anthill, then hold the magnifying glass between the anthill and the light of the sun, adjusting it up and down until the magnifying glass would turn the light of the sun into a concentrated beam of pure heat. A beam my grandfather would then use to incinerate the ants on the ground…"

"I like that analogy," interjected Beck with a growing smile. "Except the human scum we target on Earth has much less value to me than those poor ants."

"Precisely," agreed the general. "With regard to that targeting, each of our three Prometheus satellites are essentially three weapons in one. The first being a mega-gigawatt thermal beam version of that magnifying glass beam. That concentrated beam will hit the target with about ten thousand degrees Centigrade of heat. As a comparison, the flame from an oxyacetylene torch is about three thousand degrees Centigrade. Hell will be cooler than what we hit them with."

All gathered laughed in eager anticipation of that prediction.

"The next is a mega-gigawatt, highly concentrated microwave beam. We will cover the Earthlings in the highest doses of radiation ever. And last, a super-high-frequency laser which, for all intents and purposes, will act as a laser cannon. All powered eternally by the sun. Because of the orbit around the Earth we have selected, each Prometheus weapon can cover an entire hemisphere or more and instantly burn, radiate, or vaporize its targets."

"And remind me," said Beck as he looked at the watch on his left wrist, "of the initial targets we have selected."

"Yes, my Reichsführer. Aside from the missile and rocket bases mentioned, we have targeted the major nuclear and hydroelectric plants in the United States and the rest of North America, as well as in Europe, Russia, China, Australia, and parts of South America. Additionally, we have targeted the major railway lines in those countries. And finally, for purposes of pure enjoyment and terror, we have targeted iconic government and public buildings—such as the Capitol Building in Washington, the Empire State Building in New York City, the Vatican, the Eiffel Tower, the Taj Mahal, Saint Basil's Cathedral in Red Square, and the Great Pyramid of Giza— for *complete* destruction. After just the first wave of our attacks, eighty percent of the people of Earth will be without communication, power, food, running water, and morale. Soon after that, the starvation, food riots, and barbarism will begin as they kill each other off to...*survive.*"

Reichsführer Beck stood up and meticulously adjusted his uniform as he scanned the faces of everyone in the room. When he was done, he turned back to Betz.

"Well, Hans. No time like the present. Launch the first wave of the attack."

# 44

Susan Randall ran the fingers of her right hand through her stylishly short salt-and-pepper hair as her mind flipped through every single nightmare scenario possible.

As the head of the president's Secret Service detail, Randall was generally on edge. Since the current events, it was as if she had been hardwired directly to the core of a nuclear power plant.

As President Garcia addressed the nation for the third time, the olive-skinned Randall stood off to the right of the podium in the White House pressroom and fidgeted continually. Beneath the navy-blue pants suit perfectly tailored to fit her still impressive forty-eight-year-old body, Randall kept adjusting her walkie-talkie. Then the earpiece in her left ear and the microphone attached to the end of her right sleeve attached to the walkie-talkie. And then, finally, her Glock 19. Once done adjusting her service weapon, she would subconsciously start the whole process over again.

Randall understood that the very world was facing a potential threat of cataclysmic proportions. A literally unearthly horror story evolving by the minute.

As a former naval intelligence officer who was deployed twice to Afghanistan and assisted SEAL Teams in numerous combat operations there, she understood the threat of impending death and destruction all too well.

She understood, but, in this particular case, could not care in the macro sense.

Her job...her entire being...was about protecting the life of one person. The woman now at the podium trying to reassure and comfort not only four hundred million Americans but the other over seven-and-a-half billion people on the planet.

One being her son Michael, who was now a junior at UCLA.

Randall chose not to get married after becoming pregnant. Although she liked the father as a friend and an occasional overnight guest in her bedroom, she did not love him.

They amicably went their separate ways, and it was just her and Michael for the next twenty years.

Last year, Michael came back to the DC area for Christmas and was Randall's guest for the White House holiday party. As she and Michael were standing in line to have their photograph taken with the president, Garcia had looked over at Randall, waved, and held up one finger asking her to wait a minute.

Thirty seconds later, the president walked over, hugged Randall, and introduced herself to Michael. She then asked him if he had ever had a tour of the White House. When he said no, she smiled over at Randall and said, "Well, we can't let you go back to school without a proper tour. Please allow me to be your personal guide. As soon as my duties are finished here, meet me in the West Wing Lobby. I believe your mom knows the way."

She not only gave Michael a tour of the West Wing and White House, she then invited the both of them upstairs to the presidential residence to join her and her children for a cup of eggnog and a plate of cookies shaped like various DC landmarks.

What a difference a year makes.

After dialing her over one hundred times the night before, Michael was finally able to reach his mom at her condo at the River Place complex in Rosslyn, Virginia. He let her know that he was okay, telling her, "I will be fine. I am going with my roommate and his family to their fully stocked—and armed—cabin in the San Gabriel Mountains. They have a sat phone there, and I will call you when I am situated. So…please don't worry about me. Please. Take care of my friend the president and I will see you soon. I love you, Mom."

As Randall continued to watch the president—and fidget—she took a deep breath and reminded herself she could only control the things she could control. Michael was three thousand miles away but with good people heading to a good place. While she would never stop worrying about him for one second, she had to focus the remainder of her thoughts on protecting the woman before her.

Randall had known combat. She had taken down previous threats to the life of the president. But this was different. There was no precedence for this. No nightmare recorded that could act as a blueprint.

Something…someone…descendants of Nazi war criminals… whatever…on the moon…*on the moon*…had succeeded in detonating three nuclear weapons on Earth. The bits and pieces Randall was hearing as she and her team made every preparation possible to protect "Yellow Rose" was that these beings might have the capability to take out all of our satellites, end modern life as we know it, and much worse.

Like everyone else, Randall was now operating from the worst-case model. Only, there were no real steps to follow.

She knew, to protect the president, she was going to have to invent her own steps.

What's the best protection, she asked herself, when there may be *no safe spot* on the planet Earth?

No sooner did she ask herself the question than the answer flew into her mind.

"Of course!" she unintentionally exclaimed out loud, causing the president to pause for a split second to look in Randall's direction before continuing on with her remarks to the world.

Randall then reached behind her deputy to touch the arm of National Security Advisor Peter McNamara.

When he turned to look at her, she leaned close to him and whispered, "I need to speak with you the second POTUS concludes her remarks. It's urgent."

\* \* \*

Two minutes after President Garcia was done speaking in the pressroom, Randall and McNamara were seated in the Situation Room.

"What's up, Susan?"

"For lack of a better phrase, my Spidey senses are tingling like crazy. We need continuity of government and I need to keep POTUS alive. For whatever reason, I have this *very* bad feeling—which I can't really explain or defend—that there is nowhere and no facility on Earth where we can keep her safe. None."

McNamara closed his eyes for a moment and spoke.

"Don't worry about explaining or defending very bad feelings. Those feelings are now living rent-free in all of our heads."

McNamara then opened his eyes.

"So, if there is no place safe on Earth, then that would seem to pretty much rule out surviving an attack."

Randall allowed herself a half smile. "I said *on* Earth. I think we need to dial up Vice Admiral Charles Presley right this second."

McNamara conceded himself a full smile. "As in, the commander of all of our submarine forces."

"As in *that* dude."

McNamara stood up. "Let's go talk to the president."

# 45

As the towering nurse looked  down at the unsettled eyes of Oberth, then over to the swine American, and then back at the weakling doctor, she tightened her grip on her weapon.

As she was contemplating taking it out, the red emergency phone on the wall began to shriek.

She relaxed her grip on the pistol, took her hand out of her pocket, and double-timed it the four steps to the phone.

"Yah," she barked out as she answered the phone. "Infirmary."

While listening, her eyes grew wider as her face seemed to soften in happiness.

"Yah. Bring her. We will prepare."

As soon as the nurse hung up, she began to dial the phone. Oberth knew the four digits by heart. It was the emergency number for the Lunar Gestapo.

"The American bitch apparently tried to kill herself by cutting her wrists on an exposed screw in her cell," she said to whoever answered the phone. "They are bringing her here now…. Yah. Of course. I will be here and report back."

The nurse then hung up before walking slowly over to look down intently at the strapped-down male American patient.

After several more seconds of looking, the imposing assistant turned her attention to Oberth.

"Well, Doctor. You will have another patient in a matter of minutes. Soon after that, I suspect you will have a much more important guest."

* * *

THE GESTAPO INFORMANT NURSE was wrong. She was expecting Gestapo boss Hadler.

Reichsführer Beck not only kicked the door open minutes later but this time knocked it off its hinges with the force of his fury.

As the door loudly clattered to a stop one foot from Stewart's bed, two things of immense consequence happened at precisely the same moment.

Despite his orders from Oberth, Stewart's eyes snapped open with the violent entrance. As they did, Beck threw the object that was dangling from his right hand.

To the absolute horror of Oberth and Stewart, they both recognized it immediately. It was a human head.

The nurse watched the head come to rest under one of the other two examining tables in the room before turning to look at the Reichsführer with unbridled adoration.

"That guard had one job to do!" Beck screamed so loud that it actually hurt Stewart's ears. "*One*. Make sure the American woman did not harm herself. Fortunately for him, I have relieved him of all of his responsibilities for life."

With blood still dripping from his hand, Beck jumped the ten feet between him and Stewart's bed.

"So, pig," yelled Beck as he madly oscillated in place. "You are both alive *and* awake. That is good. Your orchestrated performance is upcoming."

"Oh," said Stewart against his much better judgment. "Like the one I witnessed in the arena with your puppet?"

In a flash, Beck pulled a sixteen-inch dagger from the sheath on his right thigh and pressed the razor-sharp blade against Stewart's throat until it drew blood.

He then turned in a frenzy to look at Oberth and the nurse.

"Get out."

"But the American woman will be he—" Oberth tried to protest.

"Now!" screamed Beck even louder. "Treat her in the hallway or another room. Just get *out*."

As Oberth stood her ground, clearly in some kind of defiant thought, the nurse stepped behind her, wrapped her powerful forearm around Oberth's neck, and dragged the now kicking and screaming doctor out of the room and into the hallway.

With them now out of the room, Beck flipped his internal psychotic switch again and instantly reverted to what seemed to be a normal and reasoned tone.

"So, astronaut. Tell me what you *think* you know. Though I don't have much time, as I am in the process of crushing and conquering your world, I am still anxious to hear it."

"Simple," answered Stewart as he looked up at Beck. "I saw you giving instructions to your little puppet Hitler on the stage."

"Ah, yes," said Beck as he began to lean down toward Stewart. "The *puppet* word again. It is unfortunate that you demonstrate such a complete lack of respect for our leader and messiah. I trust I won't hear that word or *any* lack of respect *ever* again."

With that, Beck wrapped the still blood-splattered steel-cable-like fingers of his right hand around Stewart's throat while continually squeezing them with just enough pressure to cut off the blood flow from Stewart's carotid arteries to his brain.

As soon as Stewart passed out, Beck released his grip and stared down at him for several seconds. After a few more seconds, Beck's impatience kicked in and he leaned down and began to not so gently slap Stewart on both sides of his face until he came out of it.

"Astronaut," said Beck while looking into Stewart's still glazed-over eyes. "That was your first and last warning. Next time, I will tear your head from your body. Oh," added Beck with a laugh, "If you need proof that what I am saying is not a hollow threat, simply look under that far bed."

Stewart's mind had cleared enough to remember the gruesome image of the severed human head sliding across the floor of the infirmary. Instead of looking, he focused his eyes on Beck and wished he hadn't.

For, in the right corner of Beck's mouth was the beginning of a line of drool. The Nazi bastard was literally salivating with the thought of personally inflicting more pain and suffering.

"Now," Beck continued, "Where were we before your blasphemous language? Oh, yes. You were trying to tell me what you *thought* you knew."

Stewart was growing exponentially more tired of the insanity of it all and simply wanted it to end. Even if he had to facilitate that ending.

"Is *clone* an acceptable word?" asked Stewart as he looked toward the right hand of Beck.

"A clone," responded the Nazi in a more serious tone. "Well, *between us* of course, really a *sheep* in clone's clothing. But the most valuable sheep in our young history."

Stewart chose silence as his best option for the moment. It was obvious that, like all murderous tyrants, Beck loved to articulate his own brilliance.

"Be it our history or yours," Beck went on, "giving the people what they want has always been a winning formula. In many ways, the real Adolf Hitler of World War II was a genius. A troubled, tiny, whimpering, weakling of a genius, but one in some real ways nonetheless. One of those ways being that he did have a real gift to see into the future. He believed that, one day, science could re-create humans from their blood samples and DNA. Because of that, the scientists who fled Earth in our rockets in 1945 had such samples of his DNA. Our science has *always* been the best, astronaut. You know that. We were not only able to succeed in cloning the Führer but learned how to manipulate our own DNA, as well as the aging process."

"So you are the real power behind the clone throne."

Beck actually laughed with the remark.

"Funny, astronaut. And true. As the hated Lenin once said: '*He is a useful idiot.*' Ultimately, it was because of the real Hitler that the Fatherland lost World War II. It was crazy to go to war with Russia then, and his own generals were right to try and assassinate him. Because of that highly flawed DNA, do you think I would give that *thing* you saw on the stage—that glorified lab rat—any real power? I keep him isolated and happy with women, alcohol, and luxury and parade him out when needed. My people here believe he is the new messiah created by the hand of God to come back to lead us. Because of that, they will do *anything* that thing orders. Anything..."

"Including destroying the Earth."

"Oh, yes," Beck said with a smile as he clapped his hands together. "Especially that. Our new petri dish messiah has convinced them all that those from Earth are nothing but disease-ridden vermin who will expose them and their children to certain death. As such, they are desperate to carry out his orders. Which to them, of course, ultimately do come from God above."

"Just another cult. Simple, neat, and final."

"You *are* vermin, astronaut. You are," said Beck as he began to turn. "Look at the horrible state of your decaying planet today and the millions and even billions suffering. The wars. The poverty. The riots. The hate. The pollution. *How* are we wrong? How? The disease that is you Earthlings *cannot* be allowed to spread into the solar system...ever."

He turned and walked five feet toward the door before turning back to face Stewart.

"Your female Earth companion is about to be brought in here. She is already close to losing her mind from the 'terror' that is us. As you know, she just tried to take her own life. If you tell anyone of our conversation, astronaut, I will disembowel her alive right before your very eyes and then strangle you with her entrails. Much better you both stay alive a little longer, as I still have some need for you."

# 46

General Betz felt as if the weight of the world had been lifted off his shoulders. Well, actually the weight of *two* worlds, laughed the general to himself as he looked out across the whitish-gray lunar landscape at the bluish-green Earth cresting just over the horizon.

After eighty-four years, they no longer had to hide themselves from the scum of Earth. They no longer had to scurry along below the surface like some kind of city rats afraid to be discovered.

No more. Ever.

They rightfully announced themselves with the three nuclear weapons and would soon cause the leaders of Earth to soil themselves in terror at what was about to appear in their nighttime sky.

Three blazing Nazi Battle Stars.

Each, Betz knew, were roughly the same size as the famed Nazi battleship the *Bismarck*. A World War II ship each of them had learned about during their schooling and university on the moon.

"The most glorious battleship in the history of war," they were taught. A ship that was fired upon by the cowardly British over 2,800 times from afar and still could not be sunk.

Now, today, General Betz was proudly in charge of the most glorious of all spaceships. His Battle Stars.

Three multipurpose weapons platforms that could *never* be threatened.

Each carrying one Prometheus weapon. A weapon that, when its massive solar arrays were fully extended, would be the brightest object in the nighttime sky of Earth other than the moon Betz now stood upon.

Each Battle Star ferrying fifteen space fighters and a crew of thirty. Each fighter equipped with not only directed-energy weapons but the more "primitive" MG-17 machine guns originally built for the Luftwaffe during World War II and put to great use against the Allied enemy aircraft by the vastly superior German Messerschmitt fighters.

As the Nazi lunar weapons experts had discovered, because the cartridges of the MG-17 machine guns carried their own oxidizing agent within the shell, there was no need for atmospheric oxygen to ignite the charge. Not only could they be fired at will—with the thrust of each space fighter adjusted to compensate for Newton's third law—but each round would theoretically travel forever in space should it miss its intended target.

A theory, Betz knew, they would never get to test, as his space fighter pilots would *not* be missing their targets.

Space fighters that were docked to the Battle Stars that would soon be taking off from their hangars hidden deep within the shadows on the far side of the moon.

Battle Stars that, in approximately a day's time, would assume their offensive positions 22,300 miles above the Earth.

Betz would have preferred that, as soon as the Battle Stars released their Prometheus weapons into orbit, they would fire upon their selected and programmed targets immediately.

Reichsführer Beck had overruled him. He wanted the weapons and Battle Stars glowing in the skies of Earth at least one night to serve as instruments of fear and terror before they unleashed their fires from Hell.

So be it.

All normal and civilized life on Earth was about to end, and Betz exalted in the fact that there was nothing the Earthlings could do to save themselves.

Nothing.

# 47

Irena Oberth was back in the infirmary with her now *two* patients. But not until she herself was bloodied, bruised, and shaken…to the core.

After being dragged out into the hallway by the Amazonian-like nurse, she was fully prepared to launch what she knew would have been a futile defensive attack upon the Gestapo pawn until she saw the American woman laying still almost completely naked and clearly close to death upon the stretcher parked next to her.

Oberth then broke free from the grip of the nurse in her haste to evaluate and treat the American woman.

When the nurse realized what Oberth was doing, she stood to the side, happy not to help one bit while awaiting the Reichsführer to appear.

The first thing Oberth did was take off her lab coat and cover most of the American's exposed body. She then looked down at the haphazard bandages applied to the woman's still bleeding wrists before going about checking her vitals.

As she was doing that, Reichsführer Beck calmly emerged through the doorway. Within two seconds, he had correctly ascertained the explosive tension before him.

Had he not, the Gestapo nurse removed any doubts.

"My Reichsführer," she proclaimed as she stood at attention. "I will gladly put this subhuman American invader out of her misery at your command."

Before Beck himself could deal with the nurse, Oberth turned from her patient and leapt with all of her pent-up fury to attack her.

The nurse easily deflected Oberth's wildly flailing swings before slapping her hard across the face and down to the floor. Once there, she jumped on the doctor, put both her hands around Oberth's throat, and proceeded to choke her out.

That act of derangement lasted all of three seconds until Beck grabbed the nurse by the back of her neck and threw her twenty feet down the hallway toward his personal security detail, which had just rounded the corner.

In her confused rage, the nurse stood, put her right hand in her pants pocket, and pulled out her small pistol. An act that turned out to be the very last movement she ever made on her own.

No sooner did the major in charge of Beck's security detail see the weapon clear the nurse's pocket than he pulled his modified Luger from its holster and shot her twice in the temple.

Before the nurse could fully crumple to the floor, Oberth's scream merged with the echoes of the gunshots to fill the hallway.

Still unnaturally and eerily calm, Beck picked Oberth up from the floor, then turned to gaze down the hallway before looking down upon the now shaking doctor.

"It *appears*...you need a new nurse and...better supervision. I will have my personal physician assist you. In the meantime, call whoever you need right away to help you tend to the two Americans. Don't make me repeat the penalty for failure."

* * *

As Oberth was inserting an IV into Washington's right arm, an orderly was placing the head of the storm trooper in a plastic bucket.

After he carried the bucket out of the room, Stewart turned to look at Oberth.

"Surreal is now taking a hit from the crack pipe."

"Crack what?" asked the doctor as she went about cutting the blood-filled bandages off the wrists of Washington so she could examine the wounds and re-dress them properly.

As she turned her head slightly toward Stewart, he saw the beginning of a bruise on her face and the finger marks on her neck.

"Oh my God. What happened to you? Are *you* all right?"

"Yes, American," Oberth answered curtly. "Fine. We've got much more important things to worry about than a few bruises."

Stewart craned his neck further to look over at Washington. "Will Venus be all right?"

"Venus?" asked Oberth with a little smile in spite of the circumstances. "Like the planet? What a beautiful name."

"Well. I'm guessing the original credit goes to the Roman god of love. Then the planet got in on the act. But for the Venus you are treating, she was named by her mom after one of the most amazing tennis players in the history of the Earth."

"Thank you for telling me," said Oberth in a softer tone. "No matter who or what, it's a beautiful name for a beautiful woman."

"Yes," agreed Stewart. "Beautiful inside and out."

"*Your* woman?" asked Oberth as she turned back to her patient.

"Oh, no," chuckled Stewart. "We are just good friends. She's got *way* too much class and intelligence to be interested in someone like me."

Oberth turned and looked down at him for a three count.

"I see your point."

Stewart burst out laughing. As soon as he did, Oberth once again clamped her hand over his mouth.

"Shut up, American," she insisted as she turned toward the door.

She then turned to lean down to Stewart and removed her hand. "Quiet," she whispered.

"First," answered Stewart in a matching whisper, "it was *your* fault for making me laugh. And second, I'll shut up if you take these straps off of me."

Oberth looked at the door and then over at Washington.

"Let me finish replacing her bandages and then I will undo your straps. But you must keep them over you like they are still in place."

"Naturally."

Four minutes later, the straps still ran across Stewart's body but were no longer secured.

"*American...*"

"My name...is...Ian," corrected Stewart in his own whispered voice.

"*Ion?* Like the particle?"

"Don't make me laugh again," cautioned Stewart as he smiled up at her. "No. Ian. I-A-N. Ian. As in a very handsome and fun-loving Scotsman."

"Oh," she said with a smile. "The Scottish. The people on Earth who lived with sheep. Maybe I-A-N was the sound a sheep makes."

Stewart had always gotten silly when he was sleep deprived, and 240,000 miles from home did not seem to cure that reality.

It took him thirty seconds—and Oberth almost smothering him—to stop laughing. Stress did do strange things to people, and Stewart knew it was affecting him greatly now. Emotional pinball at its worst.

He took a deep breath and let it out slowly.

"Sorry."

Oberth snapped back to serious. "We don't have time to be sorry. We don't have time for anything. Our enemy…our *shared* enemy…is going to walk through that door any second despite your stupid comments I don't understand about 'surreal.' You don't think this is a nightmare for some of us? I told you, American. There are a few hundred of us who oppose these monsters. You don't think we know of the evil that existed in Germany during World War II? Or the atrocities they committed? We live it every day of our lives because that evil exists with us *now* here on the moon. *Our* home, American. A home where we are not wanted and are spit upon. A home we are only allowed to inhabit because we are of some use to these barbarians…"

"Irena," began Stewart, "I understand…"

"Sssshhh. You don't understand *anything*. Let me finish. Please…. There *is* a resistance. There are people willing to die to stop this new 'master race.' But they are not ready. *We* are not ready. The landings by you and the Chinese accelerated the plans of the Führer. He—"

"Irena. Please listen to me. He is not—"

"*Listen*," Oberth hissed with fear now in her voice. "We are not ready to fight them, but we have no more time. We now have to run and escape to create the time we need. The resistance has a hiding spot. A safe place. It is a lunar cave much deeper below the surface. The Nazis don't know about it. They won't find it. It is well stocked. Food. Vehicles. Weapons. A few of our people are storm troopers. Two of them are even fighter pilots. Our *only* hope to live and survive is Earth, American. Your Earth…"

Suddenly, Oberth heard voices approaching from outside in the hallway.

"*American*. There is going to be an explosion soon. Tonight. Very soon. The hallway will be sealed off. You and your Venus comrade will be taken."

Stewart reached out and held her hand. "Explosion…wait… what…what about you…"

Oberth shoved his hand back under the sheet and put the strap back over his body seconds before two storm troopers and Beck's personal doctor walked into the room.

* * *

Fifteen minutes later, Marie Oberth walked into the small windowless bedroom of the cramped three-room quarters located on the lowest and least desirable tier of the Wolf Lair. It was a poor and humble home she shared with her husband of twenty-eight years and their daughter.

She looked as if she was in a trance.

"Gottfried," she said in a whisper to the man with the thinning gray hair holding a small plastic bag of ice to his mouth and face. "That was Irena. She just called from a phone in the hallway to say it is tonight. That everything has been moved up. She said we are to bring our prepacked bag of supplies and meet her in the infirmary in four hours."

Gottfried lowered the bag of ice and looked with unrestrained love at the woman who was his very life.

"Finally," he said as he waved his wife over to come sit by his side on the bed. "Finally, my love. It is all going to be okay. We will either escape with our daughter to this safe place to await the next steps, or we will leave this life and be together for eternity. Either way, it is time."

As his wife leaned down to hug him, her eyes filled with tears. Suddenly, after thirty seconds, she leaned back with a worried look on her face.

"What if they don't let us in the infirmary?"

Gottfried laughed in pain as he pointed toward his still swelling lips and his torn and blood-oozing gums where two of his teeth had been until his assault at the hands of the storm trooper.

"I think I've got a legitimate reason to go there."

Marie smiled through her tears, caressed his swollen face, and then held him tight.

# 48

Virtually every telescope on Earth and every camera in every satellite orbiting the Earth were now pointed at the moon.

But, the moon is indeed a very large body, and you still can't see what doesn't want to be seen.

Until it does.

A space operations officer detailed to the Air Force Space Command headquartered at Peterson Air Force Base in Colorado Springs, Colorado, was the first to see them.

Monitoring several satellite feeds at once, his eyes flicked from screen to screen until movement on the sixty-inch flat screen to his left caused them to stop flicking.

A screen that was filled by a greatly magnified section of the moon. A section that now seemed to have three tiny black dots moving fairly quickly above the bright white-gray surface of the moon.

Only, the space operations officer knew that the black dots could not be tiny. Based on the scale within the screen, they had to be enormous.

He quickly isolated them, tagged them, and then let his software do the rest.

Each object was approximately one thousand feet long and over a hundred thousand tons, and following a trajectory that would place them in an orbit around the Earth.

The officer next pushed a button on his console to activate all hell breaking loose at the Space Command. A state of being that was about to go global.

* * *

THIRTY-TWO MINUTES AFTER THE OBJECTS were spotted, the X-39 that was mated to the Titan III C booster screamed off its launchpad at Vandenberg Air Force Base to join the other that was already increasing its altitude in orbit to intercept whatever was Earth-bound.

As that was happening, crews were frantically preparing the remaining ten X-39s for flight and…the fight.

* * *

CAROLINA GARCIA WAS TRULY COMING TO HATE the Situation Room at the White House. If they survived all this, she fully intended to have it turned into a small art gallery featuring only paintings of kittens, puppies, baby seals, and any other fluffy things that wouldn't destroy humanity.

In the meantime, here she was…again.

"What do we *actually* know?" asked the president of those gathered around the table.

"Not much, unfortunately," answered the secretary of defense.

"Wait," said the president as she looked at the faces. "Where is Colonel Richards?"

"When the objects were detected," answered Jensen, "he requested permission to fly back to Vandenberg immediately so he could command the X-39 fleet."

"And obviously," replied Garcia as she looked over at an empty chair, "you gave him that permission."

"He's the best we have in the country, Madam President," interjected Tim Shannon. "We need him up there."

To Jensen, McNamara, and everyone else in the room, it still rang odd that Shannon called his significant other, "Madam President."

For Shannon, it was the only title to use in public. He remembered once reading that Bobby Kennedy, even after he became the attorney general of the United States, would still only call his brother John "Mr. President" in public. Shannon felt that if that standard was good enough for Bobby Kennedy and President John F. Kennedy, it was damn sure good enough for him.

Garcia nodded at Shannon as she took one more look at the empty chair. Though she surely would miss his expertise by her side, she agreed that his place was in Earth orbit looking to create any kind of edge.

"Back to the objects," continued the president. "Was Colonel Richards' guess wrong? Is everything wrong? Are they capable of landing on Earth? Are they carrying weapons? Spacecraft? What?"

"I think we have to prepare ourselves for any and all of those contingencies," answered Jensen.

"With all due respect, Mike," said Shannon, "I don't agree with that."

Shannon, in fact, did have a great deal of respect for the SecDef. But at the same time, he also knew that Jensen's military and civilian career was dedicated to law enforcement and not military combat, air combat, or human spaceflight.

"Tim?" asked the president in a tired voice.

"To me…and without repeating all the mistakes and questionable political positions Colonel Richards outlined earlier…these savages already have the high ground. They have it. Again, at least as far as the United States is concerned, we were in the process of ceding that ultimate high ground to the Chinese, anyway. These people simply took it from all of us."

"And your point is…" queried Jensen.

"My point is," answered Shannon as he took a quick look at Garcia, "that they are already in an almost unbeatable position of strength. They don't need to take risks such as trying to enter our atmosphere. Maybe they can, maybe they can't, but as far as I'm concerned, who cares. They *won't*. As discussed, they can fairly easily take out all of our satellites and then, once done with that, simply start taking potshots at us. It will be like shooting fish in a barrel for them."

"Take potshots at us with *what*? What does all of that *mean*, Tim?"

Shannon could hear the worry entering the president's voice, and it truly made him sad. President or not, she was still a mom who was deeply concerned for the safety of her own children.

"I'm sorry, Madam President. It means that if I were them, I would set up shop in geosynchronous orbit and then systematically start to drop nuclear bombs all over the planet."

"But Colonel Richards said he believed they didn't have the ability to get their craft through the heat of our atmosphere and hit a designated target."

"He may be right, but they might be able to get some unguided weapons through our atmosphere and detonate them indiscriminately over land."

"I'm sorry," said President Garcia with the first real display of anger any of them had heard, "but that's not good enough. It's simply *not*. This is *all* speculation at this point. All of it. Colonel Richards. You, Tim. *Doomsday* weapons. The reams of fantastical scenarios flowing in from our various three-letter agencies by the minute. Just pure speculation or 'educated' guesses. Other than being positive that this enemy to humanity is on the way, we have no idea what they might do next. None. Correct me if I'm wrong. Anyone."

Awkward silence from the table met her challenge.

President Garcia slowly stood up and looked at those gathered around her. Good people doing the best they could while operating from the dark.

"I am going to take a quick walk in the Rose Garden. I need a breath of fresh air."

# 49

Ian Stewart heard a cough and then turned to see that Venus Washington was wide awake and staring at the ceiling.

"Where am I?" she asked in a raspy voice.

"On the moon."

"No shit. Where?"

"In some kind of clinic or infirmary. The doctor…"

Just then, Irena Oberth walked back into the room, and Washington let out a quick and startled scream.

Oberth ran over and put her hands on Washington's shoulders. Both women were about the same size, and Oberth was having trouble holding down the now hysterical Washington.

Stewart slid off his bed and put his right hand over Washington's mouth. "Venus. Venus. It's me. It's okay. She's your doctor. She's a friend. She's the one who has been treating you."

Oberth was beginning to think that *she* was going to lose her *own* mind any second. A crazy woman on the bed. An arrogant and stupid man out of his bed and putting them all at risk. And an act of violent rebellion about to happen in minutes.

"Get back into the bed, American. Now," Oberth demanded through clenched teeth as she held down the still struggling Washington.

"But you need help," pointed out Stewart as he turned to look into her dark, non-Germanic, and pleading eyes.

Truly beautiful eyes, thought Stewart for the first…and at the worst…time.

"No, I don't. Look at her. She is calming down."

Stewart looked and Washington had completely stopped fighting. He then removed his hand.

"None of this can be real," Venus whispered out loud to herself as she began to laugh. "None of this can be real. None of it. I'll wake up from this nightmare soon."

Stewart hurried back into his bed and pulled the straps back over his body. First, because he had to. And second, because he suddenly didn't want the woman with the dark, beautiful eyes to be upset with him.

"Shouldn't you give her a sedative or something?" Stewart asked Oberth as he smoothed down the straps.

"No," answered Oberth as she looked down at the now smiling and clearly not quite there mentally Washington. "I need her to be able to walk and run in a few minutes. *We* are going to need that."

"Irena. Before whatever happens is about to happen, I need to tell you something about your Führer…"

"First," stated Oberth as she whirled around to face Stewart. "He's not *my* Führer. He's my shame. The shame of our world here. And second, we have heard the rumors, American. We have seen the signs. Talking about that now gets us nowhere. Survival comes before all else."

At that very moment, a storm trooper moved the blanket Oberth had hung in place of the door Beck had kicked off and shoved a man and a woman into the room. The male was holding a small bag.

"You have a new patient, Doctor," announced the sneering sergeant. "And his petrified mouse of a wife. I believe you know them."

Oberth's parents stood meekly just inside the room until the storm trooper left.

Once he did, they stood straight and proud and rushed over to hug their daughter.

"Papa!" exclaimed Irena. "Are you all right?"

"Just another badge of honor," answered her father as he offered a teeth-missing smile.

"Oh my goodness," said Marie Oberth as she took a step toward the hospital beds. "Are those the American Earth people? What have those monsters done to them…to you two…I am so sorry."

As both Stewart and Washington looked at a somewhat older but just as beautiful version of Irena Oberth, the doctor spoke in German.

"They don't speak German, Mama. They will be fine if we can get them out of here. If we can get *all* of us out of here."

Just then, several loud shots rang out in the hallway. Immediately afterward, it sounded as if two large bags of potatoes had hit the concrete after a ten-story fall.

Just as suddenly, the blanket covering the door was thrown open again and two new storm troopers entered the room. Each holding a pistol in their right hands. Each pistol still giving off hints of faint white smoke from the barrel.

Stewart climbed off his bed and got into a fighter's stance. While still woozy in the head, he was not about to be shot while lying in a bed assumed to be some weakling American chicken.

As he was preparing his mind for his final conflict, he heard the name "Peter" yelled out.

He then watched as Irena Oberth ran across the room and threw her arms around the larger of the two very large and clearly fierce storm troopers.

*What...*blinked Stewart to himself.

After the hug, the storm trooper spoke quickly in German to Irena.

She then turned and looked toward the confused Americans.

"He says we have to go...*now.*"

She then turned to look at her parents. "Mama and Papa. Help me with the Earth woman. She has lost a great deal of blood and is still weak."

Her parents walked over and began to help Washington out of the bed.

As they did, Irena went over to a locker in the far corner, opened it, and took out two blue jumpsuits similar to the one she was wearing as well as two pairs of generic black boots. She gave one set to her parents so they could assist Washington in getting into them, and gave the other set to Stewart.

After Stewart got in, put on the boots, and zipped up the suit, he looked down at himself.

"Not bad," he remarked of his new look.

At that, the two storm troopers began to laugh out loud, and the one called Peter said something under his breath to his comrade, which elicited even more laughter.

"Am I missing something?" asked Stewart with a frown.

"Yes," Irena said, smiling. "Those suits are made for the women here on the moon, and the larger of the two soldiers said it looks like 'a perfect fit' on you."

"Whatever," said Stewart as he shook his head and let out a deep breath.

The storm trooper named Peter then began to wave them urgently toward the door.

When they got into the hallway, Stewart saw two dead Nazi storm troopers on the floor, as well as two other large men down the hallway setting what looked like explosive charges.

The big storm trooper pointed them in the opposite direction of the explosives. As they all hurried down that section of the hallway, the two men setting the charges finished with their task and ran to join them.

As the now nine of them reached the far end of the hallway, the lead storm trooper directed them through a door to the left. When Stewart stepped through, he found himself standing with the others on a platform leading to a narrow metal staircase that seemed to go down forever to the very bowels of the moon.

The storm trooper spoke to Irena as he showed her some kind of device now in his hand.

She anxiously nodded her head and then motioned everyone to follow her down the staircase.

As they all began to walk down the staircase, the lead storm trooper stayed behind.

"He's waiting for us to get a safe distance away before he deto-nates the explosives that were placed. There is only one entrance to the wing the little clinic was in, and those explosives will cave in all of it and hopefully give us the time we need to get away and join the others waiting at the resistance base."

No sooner did she finish the words than there were two massive ear-shattering bangs. The staircase they were on began to shake so violently that Stewart and everyone else had to grab the railings with both hands and hope it did not separate from the wall and send them all crashing to a bottom he could not see.

After what seemed like an eternity, the shaking stopped and everyone started to breathe again. Twenty seconds after that, the big storm trooper called Peter reappeared as he pushed Stewart aside to assume the lead position.

Stewart was on edge as much as he had ever been in his life, and close to flat-out *crazy*.

As such, his kneejerk reaction was to rush forward and kick the storm trooper down the staircase to hoped-for oblivion. As he started to go down the stairs two at a time to launch his kick, he just as quickly forced himself to stop. They clearly needed that guy to escape. He then counted to ten mentally and took several deep breaths. Once done, he tried to locate Irena in the line of people slowly continuing down the stairs toward the blackness of whatever hope may lay below.

As he walked silently down the endless stairs behind them, her face…and condescending yet playful teasing…filled his mind.

*That would be something*, he thought with a small smile as he picked up the pace.

\* \* \*

THE EXPLOSIONS SET OFF in the wing housing the private clinic were heard and felt throughout much of the Wolf Lair.

Reichsführer Beck, who rarely slept more than four hours a night, was in his private quarters meeting with Hadler and Betz. Everything was proceeding exactly to plan.

A development that generally made Beck exceedingly nervous.

As his quarters shook from the first blast waves of the explosions, Beck looked at the head of the Gestapo and his top general in exasperation.

"The Americans," he spit out.

Hadler and Betz knew better than to speak at the moment. Beck was capable of anything when consumed by anger and hate, and neither had any intention of getting in the way of the outlet for all that rage.

Two minutes later, the captain in charge of security for that section of the Wolf Lair knocked at the door to Beck's private quarters and was then admitted by the major in charge of Beck's security detail.

The captain and major exchanged a very knowing look as the captain walked into the living room of Beck's large and opulent quarters.

"My Reichsführer," began the captain as his voice quivered just an octave. "There has been an explosion in the section housing the Americans."

Beck nodded slowly as he stood.

"Have you been able to reach the guards in that section?"

"No, my Reichsführer. We've tried repeatedly by radio. At the moment, we can't get into that section because the debris is blocking us."

"I see," answered Beck quietly as he continued to nod his head.

"My apologies, my Reichsführer."

Beck now shook his head and put his left hand on the shoulder of one of his most valued young officers.

"Nonsense, Captain," reassured Beck in his same flat monotone voice. "What could *you* do?"

The captain relaxed internally and looked for a second toward the major, only to see that the man was staring at the floor in clear distress.

"Please," continued Beck as he put his left hand in the small of the captain's back and directed him toward the front door of his quarters. "Allow me to walk you out."

When they reached the hallway, Beck simply nodded.

The captain saluted and began to walk away. When he was ten feet down the hallway, Beck called out to him.

"Oh, and captain. Please let me know if you hear anything…"

At that exact second, Beck emptied the entire magazine of the pistol now filling his right hand into the torso of the large storm trooper.

"...from *Hell!*" screamed Beck at the top of his lungs as spittle flew from his mouth.

He stormed back into his quarters and stared through a red haze at the major in charge of his security detail.

"Get someone to clean up that pile of shit lying out in the hallway...*immediately.*"

He then turned to face Hadler and Betz.

"We complete this mission. We *complete* it. I want that planet burned to its core. Men, women, and children incinerated. All of them. No mercy. None."

"Yes, my Reichsführer," they both answered in unison.

"Then I want the Americans and the traitors who helped them to escape caught. I want them all alive. Especially the Americans. No one kills them but me. No one. I am going to personally torture them for days. One at a time in front of the others."

"Yes, my Reichsführer," they both answered again.

"Go!" screamed Beck as he threw his now empty pistol through the flat screen monitor on the far wall of his living room.

# 50

Based upon a hurried conversation between the secretary of defense, the head of NASA, and the vice chairman of the Space Corps—then approval by the president—one X-39, which had already been in orbit when the Earth was attacked, was now in a parking orbit 22,300 miles above the United States.

Major Juanita Martinez occupied the pilot's seat, while Captain John Harper was the tactical officer. They had already been in orbit for a month and desperately wanted to get back to Earth, their families, and a hot shower.

The fact that Vandenberg had just told them another X-39 would soon dock with them to resupply essentials was not a good sign.

Both Martinez and Harper were very good at shifting mental gears, and accepted the fact they were going to be on station for many more days yet to come. They knew they were two pawns in a game they did not control.

They also knew that they, and through them the world, were in the worst and quite possibly most untenable position ever. Rather than think about it nonstop and drive themselves crazy, both accepted that they had a critical job to perform. A job that most likely came with a preordained fate.

Both chose to accept that fate and go back to arguing their favorite subject.

"Moron," said Martinez with a smile as she looked at Harper. "Have you ever even *been* to a Premier League football match? Ever? Not only does its superiority prove that American football should be renamed 'throwball,' but its popularity around the world makes the NFL look like a bar league from the boondocks."

Harper pulled the straw out of his mouth that was supplying him his ice-cold contraband Coca-Cola and turned to face Martinez.

"Ha, ha, ha. Okay. Let's look at the latest scores from the Premier League. Here we go. Zero to zero. Zero to zero. Or...as they say over there across the pond...nil to nil. Sorry, *Gov-na*. Snore, snore, snore. Now, let's turn to the sports section to see the scores from last Sunday's NFL schedule.... Wow. Amazing *and* exciting. The Patriots put up forty-two points against their opponent. Dallas scored thirty-five against theirs. Kanas City racked up sixty-two. Sixty-two! That equals cheer, cheer, cheer."

"You poor, pathetic ignoramus," laughed Martinez. "Until you actually go and watch Manchester United play in person, then—"

The warning alarm for their long-range radar scanner suddenly went off and stopped the conversation and kidding cold.

"Activate live feed. Record everything," commanded Martinez as she first looked out the front window of the spacecraft and then down at her displays. "The cameras should lock onto the radar blip any second."

"Roger that," answered Harper. "It's not space junk or debris at this altitude. That's for sure."

"No way. Whatever it is, it's approaching from the direction of the moon," said Martinez as she continued to scan every screen.

"There it is," said Harper as he moved his left index finger to point at an object on one of the monitors picked up by the telescopic lens of the main camera.

"Holy shit!" exclaimed Martinez. "That thing has to be enormous. Let's call home and get them spun up."

"Vandenberg, Vandenberg. This is Badger One, over."

"Roger, Badger One," answered a somewhat metallic voice. "We are tracking it and receiving your feed and telemetry. Please maneuver continually to keep the object in front of you. Request you zoom out the main camera to take in as much space around the object as possible."

"Roger that," answered Harper. "Zooming out now."

As Harper zoomed out with the main camera, Martinez put her index finger and thumb on a tiny joystick that controlled a secondary camera and slowly zoomed in on the object. An object that was simultaneously zooming in on them simply because of distance covered.

"Are you seeing what I'm seeing?" asked Martinez as she pointed to the sides of the increasingly larger black object.

"You mean what looks like multiple space fighters docked to each side of that thing?"

"Yup."

Just as he answered, they both saw the movement. Two of the fighters had just separated from the main craft.

"Stand by, Vandenberg. Looks like we may have some company coming," said Martinez.

"Roger that, Badger One. We see them."

Harper turned to Martinez. "Damn. Is there anything in my teeth? My mom always told me to brush just in case someone shows up unexpectedly. She's gonna be really upset with me now."

Martinez laughed as she gently fired the thrusters to keep their spacecraft aligned with the looming object.

As she did, she thought about how exposed and vulnerable they truly were.

The X-39 was equipped with directed-energy weapons. But only low-level devices meant to blind or misalign hostile satellites. Namely those of the Chinese and Russians. The two nations Martinez and Harper had been war-gaming against for the last month.

Beyond that, they were totally defenseless.

"Five thousand meters and closing," reported Harper.

"Roger," answered Martinez and Vandenberg at the same time.

"Four thousand."

"I've got a very bad feeling about this," said Martinez out loud, but really to herself.

She then reached under her shirt and pulled out a thin silver chain attached to a medallion of the Virgin Mary. She kissed the face on the medallion and looked toward Harper.

"It's okay," he said as he reached for her hand. "We've got this."

He looked down at the display, but there was no need. The two fighters were now clearly visible out their front windows.

"Vandenberg," said Harper as he thought he could now make out the silhouettes of two pilots in each spacecraft. "They are holding at three hundred meters."

"Roger that, Badger One. Do not attempt any movement that could be perceived as threatening."

Martinez and Harper both laughed at the idiocy of that comment.

"Is pissing myself considered threatening, Vandenberg? Over," asked Harper with a final laugh as he picked up a still camera to take a few shots.

After taking several close-ups of the two fighters, he looked over at Martinez.

"I don't know," he began with zero conviction in his voice. "Maybe they are preparing to communicate with us or waiting for a signal."

Martinez shook her head while continuing to hold the medallion given to her by her grandmother after her first communion.

"No way. These Nazi douchebags have already dropped three nukes on our planet, I don't thi—"

Martinez never got to finish the sentence. Just then, both of the Nazi space fighters opened up with their MG-17 machine guns. Each weapon firing 1,200 rounds per minute.

Forty high-velocity bullets per second were ripping through their target.

As the cabin of the X-39 began to shred, Vandenberg heard two final words screamed out: "Fuck yooooooou...."

\* \* \*

WATCHING IT ALL PLAY OUT in real time in the Situation Room was President Garcia, her staff, and her advisors.

With that final scream of defiance still echoing in her mind, Garcia closed her eyes and wept.

After a minute, she wiped her face and looked around the room. "Okay. We know exactly where we stand now. Exactly. These people…these Nazis…these monsters…are who they have always been. They will show no mercy and take no prisoners. I now truly believe the survival of the human race on Earth is at stake. We either figure out a way to stop them or they will exterminate us all. Tomorrow, we meet with the world. Let us hope and pray there is strength in numbers."

\* \* \*

CAROLINA GARCIA SAT IN THE DARK next to Tim Shannon on the Truman Balcony overlooking the south lawn of the White House, the Washington Monument, and the Jefferson Memorial.

She saw none of those things. Her eyes were fixated on a bright light in the nighttime sky that had suddenly appeared over Washington, DC and all of North America.

"They are right there and we can't hit them," observed Garcia.

"We are going to try, Lina," answered Shannon, using his term of endearment and love for her when they were alone.

"Like those two poor pilots who were just kil…"

Garcia started to cry again. As she did, Shannon's eyes filled with tears. This was simply too much for any human mind to handle.

He got up from his chair, walked behind hers, knelt, and wrapped both of his arms around her shoulders while resting his head against hers.

"I love you, Lina."

"I love you more, my darling. I'm so sorry I put you on the spot earlier."

Shannon leaned closer and softly kissed her neck.

"You should have," he answered with a laugh. "You're the president and I'm a staff guy who didn't have the correct answers."

Garcia turned her head and kissed him on the lips.

"You're the love of my life."

"Not in there, Lina. In there I'm just part of a team that you are counting on to give you the most accurate background and intelligence so you—with the weight of the world now on your shoulders—can make the best decision possible. I'm the guy who let you down."

"No," she said as she turned to see his face framed by the ambient light of the city. "You're the man who has to give himself a break. We *all* do. We are up against an evil originating from a place that no one could have imagined. No one. We will see if our allies and even former world foes have any good news for us tomorrow."

"Actually," answered Shannon as he stood and walked to the front of her. "On that front, we did get some interesting news just about twenty minutes ago. We've heard from the defense ministers of both China and Russia, and it seems that building top-secret space fighters hidden from all other countries is suddenly in vogue these days. As it turns out, each of them has twenty ready to go."

Carolina Garcia stood and reached for Shannon's hands.

"So that's forty added to our eleven. Fifty-one space fighters against the new Nazi war machine up there."

Shannon turned his head to look up at the ominous stationary light in the sky. "Yeah…well…as of now, I'm adopting '*remember the Battle of Britain*' as our new rallying cry and motto. They kicked the shit out of the Nazi Luftwaffe then, and we will find a way to do it now."

Garcia leaned in and hugged Shannon tighter than she had ever hugged anyone before. After twenty seconds, she stepped back, turned, and looked directly at the object above.

"Star light, star bright," she said while staring daggers. "First star I see tonight. Wish I may, wish I might, see your ass go boom in the night."

# 51

Susan Randall slowly walked up and down and side to side throughout the House Chamber located in the middle of the south wing of the United States Capitol Building.

Most Americans and most of the world knew the House Chamber as the room where the president of the United States delivered her or his annual State of the Union address.

In a few minutes time, a percentage of the 440 seats on the chamber floor were going to be taken up by the leaders of the United States, Russia, China, the United Kingdom, France, Germany, Austria, Canada, Mexico, Brazil, Argentina, Israel, Egypt, Jordan, Saudi Arabia, India, Pakistan, and Australia.

Those leaders who could not attend in person would be watching and contributing via secure teleconference screens.

Sitting behind the world leaders in attendance in the House Chamber would be staff and security. Too many security teams from too many countries for Randall's comfort. As such, she had instructed her people to keep them out of her way as their *only* mission.

Much to Randall's amazement, the president—in conjunction with the leaders of Russia and China—had approved Randall's fail-safe contingency plan she had urged upon her and General McNamara.

Every street around the Capitol Building had now been cleared and secured. Every possible escape route to those streets from the south wing of the Capitol Building was mapped and memorized. And multiple helicopters were on station around the building ready to take flight instantly.

Randall's "gut feeling" cost three governments tens of millions of dollars in preparation. If she was wrong and the world didn't end, she wouldn't be able to get a job as a school crossing guard.

But every fiber of her being told her she was not wrong. That the sinister light that appeared in the nighttime sky was anything but heavenly as it sent chills down her spine.

She was convinced there was now no safe place on Earth.

* * *

THE WORLD LEADERS who had gathered at a moment's notice were in their seats in the front rows of the House Chamber with staff behind them.

As Carolina Garcia was the president of the host nation for this emergency conference, she was designated to speak first.

Both because of the historic nature of the conference, as well as the building dread within her planted by Randall and the evolving nightmare around her, Garcia had her children sitting just off to the side of the podium with Tim Shannon standing behind them.

"Ladies and gentlemen," began President Garcia as she looked down upon the eager and worried faces of the world leaders before her. "Sadly, the greatest cooperative effort ever known to humanity has been war. That reality is what brings us all here today. We are now engaged in the very first *Worlds War*. A war with an enemy that has targeted all of us. Every nation on Earth. Targeted our very planet. Whatever differences we have between us as nations—real or imagined—must be cast aside this very second so that we might combine our multiple strengths in a campaign to save humanity. Every nation, every people, every faith on Earth must become one voice screaming out in unison that this will not stand. As our respective military advisors gathered here today have advised us, complete victory against the hideous Nazi menace seemingly burrowed into the moon must now be the *only* objective of the world. Every political, scientific, military, industrial, and personal effort must be directed at defeating our..."

Garcia's voice broke for just a spilt second when she saw her children out of the corner of her eye.

"...executioners. With that one and only mission in mind, the governments of Russia, China, and the United States are preparing to launch a counterstrike to the evil that now orbits our planet. An evil which, for the moment, holds the upper hand. But an evil that, thanks to the will, passion, and genius of the global population declaring they will never succumb, will soon be vanq—"

Abruptly, the power to both Garcia's microphone and the entire building was cut. At that, several people in the audience let out a scream of fright.

As they did, an incredibly high-pitched whine sounded from the ceiling of the House Chamber. The noise was so screechingly loud that it inflicted damaging pain within the ears of all in attendance.

No sooner did Randall see President Garcia's hands go up to cover her ears than she signaled her team. She then sprinted to the podium, grabbed the president around the waist, and dragged her toward the nearest door and down a preselected escape route.

As she was being propelled down a hallway against her own will, Garcia screamed out, "My children!"

"I've got them!" yelled Shannon as a blinding white and reddish beam of fire cut down through the ceiling and instantly began to fill the House Chamber with a heat that would melt steel.

As he heard the screams of the panicked and dying behind him, he grabbed both of Garcia's children around the waist and dragged them down a hallway that was getting intolerably hotter by the step.

Within seconds, they were through a side door of the Capitol Building and into air that was anything but fresh. They were instantly hit with a rancid smell of burning material, flesh, hair, and human feces from some of the survivors who had soiled themselves in terror.

No sooner was Shannon through that door than two Presidential Protection Division agents from Randall's detail grabbed the children and began running them to a helicopter that already held Garcia, the presidents of Russia and China, and several other dignitaries.

As Shannon ran for one of the other helicopters with its rotors already twirling at full power, he turned to look behind him.

As the unearthly screeching sound continued unabated, he saw the source of the noise in its entirety. A telephone pole-size beam of brilliant white and red fire stretching up into the sky as far as the eye could see. A molten beam of death and destruction that was systematically moving back and forth across the Capitol Building, transforming the historic landmark into a flaming, incinerating pile of blackened rubble.

With fight-or-flight survival adrenaline now surging through his body, Shannon put his head down and sprinted to the door of the helicopter that now seemed to be lifting off the ground.

Three feet from the door, he launched himself into the air and landed with a thud atop the body of someone else. No sooner did he do so than the hands of Peter McNamara dragged his legs and feet away from the closing door of the helicopter that was already accelerating toward the temporary sanctuary created by the preparedness of Susan Randall.

* * *

As soon as Shannon stepped off the helicopter that had landed next to the others in a field at the Naval Air Station Patuxent River located sixty-five miles from Washington, DC, at the edge of the Chesapeake Bay, Susan Randall took him by the arm.

"Mr. Shannon," said the agent who was holding her service weapon in her other hand. "The president has asked me to escort you to her location."

That location happened to be the newest Virginia-class nuclear-powered, fast-attack, stealth-enabled submarine in the US Navy fleet.

A submarine waiting just offshore in the Chesapeake Bay next to eight other nuclear-powered submarines. Two more from the United States that consisted of another Virginia-class fast-attack submarine as well as the latest Columbia-class ballistic missile submarine.

The three from the US combined with the same compliment of two fast-attack nuclear-powered submarines and one ballistic missile submarine from both Russia and the People's Republic of China. All not only the latest and most lethal technology, but capable of going well over 1,500 feet below the surface of the ocean for months at a time without resurfacing.

An ocean that would act as a natural shield to deflect and disperse any attack from orbit.

As Randall rode out with Shannon to the submarine on a US Navy Mark VI heavily-armed patrol boat, she informed him that the other world leaders and staff who survived had been evacuated to the base and were being placed aboard various submarines. Additionally, the nine submarines already held a preselected cross-section of the experts from various nations needed to strategize a defense of the Earth.

After Shannon boarded the *Virginia*-class fast-attack sub, he was led down to the control room.

There stood President Carolina Garcia flanked by President Medvedev of Russia and President Li of China. Both men had insisted on riding with the US president rather than in one of the nuclear submarines from their respective countries.

Standing directly behind Garcia and holding on to the back of her jacket were the president's two children. Both quietly weeping in confused fear.

Shannon stepped forward just as Garcia walked into his arms. They held each other in silence for ten seconds before Garcia whispered to him, "I love you. We will find our private time later to talk and mourn."

Garcia then stepped back and opened the presidential compartment in her brain.

"First," she began as she turned to a Navy officer, "I'd like to thank Captain Resnick for hosting us on his boat."

President Garcia shifted her gaze to the woman who had yet to holster her service weapon.

"And I'd most especially like to thank Agent Randall—my friend and protector—for putting everything on the line to create this mobile submarine command post for all of us. Thank you, Susan."

Randall hurriedly holstered her weapon and bowed slightly in humble response. "It's the highest honor of my life, Madam President."

Carolina Garcia then took in and let out a very deep breath.

She knew she would never be able to entirely process the horror that had just happened...or that was yet to come.

All she could do was her job to the best of her ability for as long as life allowed.

"These submarines," she said to those in the control room, "do offer us refuge, but we need a place where we can all gather as one. A place out of the reach of those spawns of Satan and the weapons they command in orbit."

President Medvedev turned to face her.

"Indeed," agreed the Russian leader whose motherland had paid the highest and most incomprehensible price at the hands of the Nazis almost nine decades before. Precisely because of that savagery and loss, Medvedev knew that mood and morale were everything in a fight such as this.

Now was the time to offer some positive news framed by a hint of his trademark levity.

"Madam President," continued Medvedev with a small smile appearing on his tanned face. "With regard to your correct assessment and hope, I am happy to report that just prior to the attack upon your Capitol Building, my chief of intelligence reported to me that he has located *just* such a place. Over the last number of years, we have kept constant tabs on one of our most disgruntled billionaires. A man who continues to say such nasty things about me and especially our Mother Russia. Truly not a nice person. As it turns out, he—along with two of your own multibillionaires and one from Britain—built what they *thought* was a super-secret compound off the coast of Mexico. Truly imaginative. A compound, Madam President, almost one thousand feet *below* the surface of the ocean, located within a cave protected by almost three hundred feet of solid rock. Very impressive *and* very luxurious. Five star, I'm told. The facility can hold up to two thousand people for over five years without resupply. It was the *intention* of these out-of-touch billionaires to ride out the 'end of the world' there while the rest of humanity perished. Sadly for them, that plan has been permanently altered. As we speak, special operations forces from the Russian navy and army eliminated the token security team and have taken control of that facility. At present, the occupants are being evicted to a less luxurious compound in Siberia. Should we all survive the attack from the Lunar Nazis, I'm sure we can find a suitable way to thank them for their generosity and...patriotism."

President Li laughed out loud and reached over to shake the hand of Medvedev.

"Good work...*comrade*."

President Garcia looked at both men and nodded once.

"Any port in a storm," she whispered solemnly as two images almost simultaneously flooded into her mind.

The first being the incineration of the Capitol Building and the bloodcurdling screams that accompanied that barbaric attack.

That image then being instantly and thankfully shoved aside by Tim Shannon's spot-on battle cry of "remember the Battle of Britain."

As Garcia had learned, in the summer and fall of 1940 and against all odds, vastly outnumbered and outgunned British and Allied pilots prevented the "insurmountable" multi-thousand aircraft of the Nazi Luftwaffe from gaining air superiority over Britain. And in doing so, literally saved the nation from a ground invasion and certain slaughter by the Nazis.

That, President Garcia knew, *was* the template and call to battle that now had to be cemented into the spirit of every woman, man, and child on the planet.

A people who would neither yield nor surrender to the tyranny of the homicidal perversions of humanity that were now orbiting the Earth.

* * *

Emboldened by that conviction, those who now populated the nine nuclear submarines set off for the new "Atlantis"—to reconfigure the old world and establish *one* global government.

A unified government created to fight for the very survival of all on Earth.

*To be continued...*

# Acknowledgments

First and foremost, my deepest gratitude to Anthony Ziccardi for his belief in me and this project.

I would also like thank Michael L. Wilson for his wise counsel and support.

Next, my never-ending appreciation to Heather King, Devon Brown, and the entire team at Permuted Press for their amazing talent, insight, and dedication. As the cliché goes, if there are any mistakes attached to this project, they are mine, and mine alone.

I'd especially like to thank those in the space, military, and intelligence communities who walked me through some of the issues associated with this book. Who knew revealing "alleged" Nazi secrets was so complicated.

I would also like to acknowledge my brother, Jay. His love and support is boundless, and his marketing ideas remain the best.

As always, I'd like to thank Patrick Ryan Ovide (O-Vee-Dee), my "best friend in the whole wide universe" who inspires me daily.

And finally, I would like to thank my sister Janice for always being there for me, always believing in me, and for always shining a much needed and calming light during the many dark times of our childhood and lives.